Running With George

Charles Lunsford

Regal Crest

Texas

ISBN 978-1-61929-092-1

First Printing 2013

9 8 7 6 5 4 3 2 1

Cover design by Donna Pawlowski

Published by:

Regal Crest Enterprises, LLC
229 Sheridan Loop
Belton, TX 76513

Find us on the World Wide Web at
http://www.regalcrest.biz

Published in the United States of America

Acknowledgments

This book is dedicated to:

-Ed, I am forever grateful.

-The Regal Crest editing team

-Cathy Bryerose of Regal Crest for taking a chance on me

-Phyllis Davis for pestering me to finish because she had more confidence in me than I did.

-Judith Weinberg for taking up her valuable time editing my baby.

For Eltom

Some of the characters in this book are not works of fiction. They were alive and still live in my heart. They were taken away much too early. I know that heaven is a much better place with them there. The rest are figments of my imagination.

September

I WAS JUST bending over to tie the laces on my running shoes when I heard a sound behind me. I looked up and saw the finest ass and legs I have ever seen in a pair of spandex shorts run past me. As a healthy gay American man, I followed him. Looking ahead, I could not keep my eyes off him. His broad tan shoulders tapered down to slim hips and full muscular thighs.

He was running at an easy gait, a light jog, heading for the beach. It had been some time since I had done any running, in fact, it had been more than two years so I started out quite stiff and awkward. But there were no clouds in the sky, and a light breeze was coming in from the ocean; it was a perfect afternoon to jog, especially with Mr. Spandex in front of me.

From where I had started, the beach was about eight blocks away. Then from there you could go in either direction and follow the ocean for miles. I was in no condition to go for a long run but I was curious to see where he was going.

I saw that I had fallen way behind, as he was more than two blocks ahead, so I picked up speed.

When he came to the intersection, where the highway crossed, he stopped moving but kept running in place while looking at his watch. He looked both ways, then crossed the road. When I reached the intersection, there was no traffic so I too, ran across. As I had assumed, he was heading for the beach. A quick jump down a short flight of steps brought him to the hard packed sand. As I came to the steps, I saw him turn left and start running at full speed. I was not in great shape, but I was not going to let him out of my sight.

I jumped down the steps and a little twinge in my knee told me that I was going to regret that move in the morning. I turned left and ran as hard as my forty-nine-year-old body would allow. I did not see him ahead of me. I had hoped that he would go the six blocks to the edge of town, then head away from the beach, which would take me back home. I hated the fact that tomorrow I was going to hurt for nothing. I slowed down when I reached the end of the beach. I looked all around and found no sign of him.

It was fun while it lasted, but it was time to go back. Feeling dejected, I kicked at the sand and started up a small hill toward home. When I approached the other side of the hill, there he was, standing at the intersection. When he saw me approaching, he looked at his watch.

"If you are going to chase me, you are going to have to do a better job than that," he challenged, motioning to his watch.

I stopped in front of him, taken aback. I did not know how to respond. He smiled and the corners of his hazel eyes crinkled. His thick eyelashes looked like he was wearing mascara. I felt immediately at ease.

He held out his hand. "Hi, my name is George."

I took his hand. "Chester," I replied.

"Chester?"

"My name is Chester, but everyone calls me Chick."

"Chick?"

"Yeah, it seems that I was born with a full head of yellow hair, and I looked like a baby chicken." As I said this, I could feel the blood rushing to my cheeks.

"Nice to meet you... Chick," he said smiling and still holding on to my hand.

The light turned green, and we slowly ran across the highway and down the street. On our way, we gave one another an extremely brief history of ourselves. I had lived in the town for more than fourteen years. He had lived here for five. I told him that I had started out as a hairdresser and massage therapist, but now I was the director of a large spa on Miami Beach, called The Spa. He was a recruiter for Miami Dade Fire and Rescue. I found out that he spelled his name Jorge, like the Latin version, but he preferred the English pronunciation. Since George was my grandfather's name, I obliged.

We came to the end of the street and rounded the curve to the right when I slowed down.

"Why are you stopping?" George asked.

"This is where I live," I answered.

"You're kidding," he said with a snicker. "I live at the end of the street. On the corner actually."

I could not believe my good luck. Not only did I find a handsome man to go running with, but he was almost my next-door neighbor too. Maybe something else could come of this.

"Can we do this again?" he inquired.

"S-sure," I stuttered, "but I need to tell you that I am a little rusty. I have not done this for quite a while. In fact, I will be in pain for a few days. I'll see you later, okay?"

"I'll make certain of that, Chick," he said with a wink. He ran down the street toward his house. I stood on the curb and watched as his image became smaller and smaller.

The boys, Thom and Jerry, both red standard poodles, met me at the door with such exuberance that anyone would have thought I'd been gone for days.

"Easy boys," I warned. "Let's go out."

I let them out the back door as I went into the bathroom. I took off my sweaty clothes and jumped into the shower. The hot spray felt great on my body. I could not keep the image of George's body out of my mind. The way his ample butt moved from side to side when he ran. The way he looked me in the eye when he talked to me.

His dark hair was cut very short, but you could see the flecks of gray beginning to appear. I also noticed that he had little or no body hair. I didn't know if he shaved it off or whether he was naturally hairless. I, on the other hand, had true European roots; I was covered in blonde hair, most of it gray. I could thank my father for that.

What got me the most was how he held onto my hand when he introduced himself. It was warm and firm and I felt like he was never going to let go. Picturing him in nothing but tight spandex shorts, running shoes, and covered in sweat, I had an erection, my first in a long time.

Well, Chickie, old boy, I thought, looking down, *looks like you are not dead after all.*

It had been two years since Ed had passed away, and I still felt like I was living someone else's life. I got up in the morning and walked the dogs. I went to work, came home, walked the dogs, and ate dinner. I sat in front of the television with my good friend, Jack Daniels. I fell asleep. Like Bill Murray in *Groundhog Day,* I did it all over again the next day.

ED AND I were together for more than twenty years. I always told him jokingly that I had given him my youth.

Like most gay couples, we met in a bar, surrounded by friends. That let me know that we would be spending a lot of time out or entertaining, and we did host plenty of parties.

Ed had grown up on Miami Beach but found his way to DC. Six months later, we met and it was love at first sight. We even invited his parents, Aurora and Albert, to come visit us in DC.

Ed had come out to his parents when he was a teenager and the only thing that his Cuban parents said to him was that the lifestyle that he had chosen for himself would leave him a lonely old man.

"Mom," Ed had said to his mother when he introduced me, holding her tiny hands in his. "Remember when you said I would be lonely? I want you to meet the man that won't let that happen."

His mother, Aurora, had smiled at me and walked across the room to kiss me on the cheek.

That is when I became a member of Ed's family. We would

travel often to Miami Beach, usually to party but also to visit with his folks. One day, sitting on the beach on a particularly beautiful day, and with my defenses down, I declared, "I could live here."

"I'm glad you said that," Ed responded, putting his arms around me, "because I want to come home."

And so we did.

The move was easy as moves go. The day was beautiful and sunny and, in the morning, a tall blonde woman in a smart pink Chanel suit rang our doorbell. She was from a company called Moving is a Drag and she was all business. It turned out to be our friend Thomas in drag and he made a checklist of all the important things that we needed to keep, like ball gowns, high heels, bird seed tits and, of course, vodka. With his help, we sold everything that we wanted to sell and whatever did not fit in the moving van, we left on the curb in front of the house.

Our lesbian friend, Sandi, was in charge of loading the van. She told us where to place everything, and we did what we were told. Let me explain. Sandi is a big girl and when she tells you to do something, you just do it. For example, she had three young helpers who we referred to as The Nazi Hookers. I never was sure how they got that name but that is what they were called. During the afternoon, Sandi told them to go upstairs and take their clothes off, bend over, and stick their asses toward a camera. She wanted a picture to show us that they had worked their asses off for us.

Sandi had the van packed so perfectly that there was no extra space for anything. We joked that we had to take the dirt out of the vacuum cleaner to get the van door to close. Once the door was closed and locked, we were off, never to look back.

WE FOUND A fixer-upper, that I am still fixing up, in a sleepy little town called Sea Breeze. We affectionately refer to it as Mayberry by the Sea. With the ocean on the east side and the intra-coastal waterway on the west, it is completely surrounded by water. It is located just north of Miami Beach but it could be a million miles away.

Over the years, all of Miami Beach has been referred to as South Beach by the rich and trendy, but only the part that is south of fifth street is truly South Beach. Every now and then, you will see, very early in the morning, someone pulled over for speeding by two or three police cars, and you know by their clothes, or lack of clothing, that they have been at the clubs on the beach.

We have a saying here: How many Sea Breeze police does it take to write a ticket? The answer: all of them.

Occasionally, someone will be arrested for shoplifting from the local grocery store, or a couple of young people will be picked up for drinking and fooling around on the beach late at night, but, for the most part, Sea Breeze is a quiet town and people enjoy living here. We liked it as soon as we arrived. Each house is different from its neighbor, and some have been renovated beautifully. When walking the dogs or riding your bike, there is always someone to wave hello to or stop and have a chitchat with.

Driving home from work, crossing the bridge, and heading into Sea Breeze, the ocean is on your left and the bay is on your right. They are both brilliant emerald green, and no matter how horrible your day has been, one look at the water and all your problems go away.

THE FIRST FEW years in Florida were heartbreaking. First, we lost Thomas, who we had named our dog after, to AIDS. Thomas was tall, blond and beautiful. Dressed as a man or a woman, he would turn heads. Then there was Jorge, the pediatrician. He was so handsome that women told him they would have a baby just so he could be their doctor. When joking, he would pronounce his name different ways. Sometimes it would be George, the conventional way, or like Jorge, which sounds like hore-hay. And, best of all, whore-gay, because as he would say, "I'm a whore and I'm gay."

They found him dead on the floor of his apartment the day after his thirty-ninth birthday. I think that some gay men never want to get old. Albert and Jorge were living together for a while before Jorge died. They both had a thing for one another when we all lived in DC, but neither one acted on it. Jorge said he was a whore and Albert didn't like it, so he moved out.

Then Albert was diagnosed with stomach cancer. The surgeons cut him from breastbone to navel to find the cancer. He healed nicely, and I told him the scar looked kind of sexy. He liked that. Our hopes were crushed when the cancer returned and Albert died sometime after his fortieth birthday. His family, who never spoke to him because of his lifestyle, descended on him like a flock of vultures when he got sick. They would not let us see him and thought it was best for him to leave the beach and move back to Philadelphia in the middle of the winter.

Eddie and I clung to one another for support.

"Don't ever leave me," I pleaded.

"I won't," he promised.

In DC I was a hairstylist and facialist. After working in a salon for more than twenty years, I found that I was tired of all the drama in the salon setting so I started looking for something more challenging. The opportunity arose. A large spa with a great reputation opened on Miami Beach. I submitted my resume and was hired, not as a technician but as a manager. My job was to create the format that everyone was to follow. I hired the staff and watched over the daily organization. Since I had plenty of experience in skin care and massage, I also would be required to perform these services if a technician was unavailable or sick. I worked nine to five Monday through Friday and occasionally, I would go in for a few hours on Saturday. The best part was that I could get a massage or facial anytime free of cost. This ended up being especially crucial when Ed was sick.

It was while in Greece for a cruise and tour that I first noticed that Ed did not have the energy he normally had.

"You go ahead, I'll catch up," he would say, gasping and out of breath.

On our trip back home, his feet and legs were so swollen that he had to take off his shoes. He even put his feet up on the chair back in front of him. After we landed, he could barely walk.

Months later, my family was visiting for the Thanksgiving holiday. My mother seemed worried about Ed and commented to me that he'd put on weight and seemed tired all the time.

She was right. Ed would awaken at eight in the morning and would be asleep on the sofa two hours later.

"If you don't call your doctor soon, I will call him for you," I demanded finally, pointing my finger at him.

"I will, I will," Ed whispered, "I promise."

After the holidays, I received a call on my cell phone while at work. It was Ed.

"What in the hell did you tell my doctor?" he shouted. He had never raised his voice to me.

"Eddie, don't yell at me," I said as my heart sank. "I told you that if you didn't call your doctor I would."

"Well, he wants me in his office ASAP."

"And that means when?" I asked.

"Tomorrow." He hung up.

When I got home from work the following evening, Ed's car was in the driveway.

"Honey, I'm home," I sang.

"In the bedroom," Ed responded sourly.

When I came into the room the question that was on my lips disappeared. Ed was wearing a twenty-four hour heart monitor. It looked like a harness connected to a small battery pack. Electrodes covered his chest and back.

"I failed my stress test," he confessed. "I go back tomorrow so the doctor can run diagnostics on this thing."

"Then what?" I asked sitting down next to him on the bed.

"I don't know."

WE HAD THESE beautiful Japanese goldfish that swam in a twenty-five gallon aquarium in the hallway. They had to be kept out of the sunlight because algae would take over the tank. One morning one of the fish did not look so good.

"I don't think he'll make it through the day," Ed commented, as we watched them.

"Too bad," I added. "Come on boy, you can make it," I told the fish.

"Bye, daddy," I said as I turned to Ed and kissed him. "I love you."

"I love you more," he answered back.

This was our usual routine.

Later that day my cell phone rang at work. I saw that it was from Ed and even though it was a hectic day, I answered the call.

"Yes, what is it?" I asked trying to be funny.

"Are you sitting down?" Ed asked.

"If you are calling to tell me that the fish has died, I'm sorry, but I am very busy here."

"Please sit down." His tone scared me.

"Eddie, what is it, honey?"

"I'm in the hospital."

When I arrived at the hospital and saw him in the bed, my heart sank. My big beautiful and strong husband looked like a little old man.

"The pacemaker is not working. My heart disease is too far gone. The doctors want me to have a transplant and I said no," he explained.

I walked over to the side of the bed and took his hand. He placed my hand on the side of his face. "I don't want to live like that."

"What else can we do?" I whispered.

"Pray."

I DO NOT remember much about the memorial because I was numb. I remember I rented a red Mustang convertible and my iPod was playing, "Never Can Say Goodbye," by Jimmy Somerville. I was playing it as loudly as possible with the wind blowing even louder in my ears.

As planned, I took Ed's ashes and dumped them, urn and all, off the Seven Mile Bridge near Key West. I sat there staring at the water for hours, watching the sun paint beautiful watercolors into the sea until there was nothing but blackness and stars.

When I returned to the house, the boys met me at the front door as usual. It was late, just before midnight, and I was exhausted from driving all day. When I entered the house and shut the door, the quiet was deafening. I let the dogs out and walked into the kitchen, and poured myself a large bourbon over ice. I went to the bedroom to change my clothes. I turned on the lamp on the bedside table and next to the lamp was a picture of Ed that I had taken when we were visiting Paris twenty years before. He was so young with a mustache and a head full of curly hair. I sat on the edge of the bed, drank down the contents of the glass in one gulp, and slammed it on the table.

"Why did you leave me?" I yelled at the photo. "I am so mad at you for leaving me all by myself. We were supposed to grow old together. You promised." My voice became louder.

"Now look at me. I'm left here to take care of this house and the dogs, and you are gone!" Tears of rage began boiling up inside of me. "I am so mad and hurt and alone... so fucking alone. I hate you! I hate you for doing this to us... to me!"

I threw the picture across the room where it hit the wall and broke. Glass scattered all over the floor. I fell back on to the bed and cried.

Steve and Susan, my brother and sister-in-law helped me get all of Ed's legal documents together. He left me well off. Not rich, by any stretch of the imagination, but comfortable. The house was paid for, and all I had to do was pay the utilities and the taxes. But what good was it when I had no one to share it with? I found myself sinking slowly into a black hole. It would take me almost two years of hell before I regained control of my life.

THE NEXT MORNING after meeting George the alarm and the smell of coffee woke me at five. As expected, I was sore but I didn't care. There is a pain from being overworked or being stressed out, then there is the ache from physical activity that reminds you that you are alive. I was alive and I was in a great mood. Maybe tonight I would run again. When I stood up, everything was stiff and I rethought running, for a few days at least. I hobbled out of the bedroom to the den, where the dogs were still sleeping.

"Come on boys, let's go," I ordered, opening the backdoor so they could go out. "Get a move on."

Jerry got up first and was out the door. Thom was having a little trouble getting started.

"What's wrong, old man? Are you a little stiff too? Now I

know how you feel in the mornings," I said to him as he slowly walked out the door.

It had been some time since I had gotten out of bed in a good mood, filled with so much positive energy. I felt like a different person.

I went to the kitchen, opened the fridge, and took out the evaporated milk and poured myself a big cup of coffee, adding the milk. I headed back to the bedroom to put on some clothes so I could walk the dogs. I stopped in front of a mirror and looked at myself. I was disappointed. I had always been thin, but now I had a flabby paunch that hung over what used to be my waistline.

"When did you get so old?" I asked my reflection. I stepped closer to the mirror. When did I start going gray? How did those tiny lines appear at the corner of my eyes? To hell with that, where did those dark circles come from?

"We are going to have to do something about this," I declared, grabbing my soft stomach. Aches or no aches, I had a new running friend and I was determined to get my sorry ass in shape. I turned my backside to the mirror and agreed. Yes, my sorry ass indeed.

I changed into shorts, sneakers, and a long sleeved sweatshirt. I attached the leashes to the dogs and out the door we went.

I had forgotten how dark it is at five thirty in the morning. There were hardly any lights on in any of the houses we walked by.

Even though both my dogs are the same breed, they could not be more different. Jerry, the youngest, was always in front, pulling me along. Thom had to sniff and urinate on everything. I was constantly being pulled in two different directions, I'm sure I often looked like a soft pretzel.

I decided to take a different route than we had been taking for a while and ended up in front of the house that George told me he lived in. I could see inside the house because the light was on, and I saw him go into the kitchen.

"Looks like you are a morning person, too, George," I observed, walking by the house, not even questioning why a single man would have three cars in his driveway.

THE PEOPLE WHOM I work with are truly therapists. They knew exactly what to do for me the weeks and months after Ed's death. They gave me room when I needed it, and let me talk when I felt that there was no one to talk to. Best of all the massage and treatments prescribed kept me somewhat sane. I still did my daily routine at work and at home, but I felt like I was living life at a distance.

I walked into one of the massive buildings known as The Spa.

There were three buildings in all, and the complex spanned one whole city block on the beach. From my parking space in the underground lot, I took the elevator to the third floor, which opened onto the lobby. It was two stories tall and designed in white and gray marble with a sea foam green, terrazzo floor. Large windows looked out onto the pool and ocean beyond. The treatment rooms and offices were off to the left. I walked down a warmly lit hallway with a cascading water wall. At the very end was my office. Soft music played through speakers on the floor that resembled rocks. The whole day everyone at work knew something was different about me and not just because I was walking stiff like the Frankenstein monster.

I ran into one of the massage therapists, Greg, who had helped me through my rough time. He was in his mid-thirties and like most men his age, he shaved his head and sported a goatee. He had a stocky build and big, strong hands.

"Greg, you've got to help me," I pleaded.

"What have you done?" he asked.

"I hurt myself," I paused, then whispered, "running."

"You, running?"

"Don't sound so surprised," I imparted, "I think I'm back among the living."

"Hallelujah!"

Greg was sexually ambiguous and never spoke of a girlfriend but always talked about the guys. It was not my job to ask questions about anyone's preference. I was out at work, and I thought everybody who was gay should feel comfortable to do the same. All I knew was that Greg was a master of massage and if anybody could get the kinks out, it would be him.

"You know Chick, for a man who's almost fifty, you're not in bad shape," Greg snickered.

"Thanks," I sighed. I was lying on my stomach on the massage table with my face in the face cradle. "I look like shit, but you don't have to make it sound like the kiss of death."

"You know what I mean. When was the last time you worked out?" he asked.

"It's been awhile. The last time I went to the gym, some guy blew me in the shower."

"Here?" Greg asked sounding a bit too interested.

"No, not here."

"Why don't you work out here? It's great. Me and the guys use it all the time."

"I never thought about using the gym here."

"Chick, sometimes I wonder where your brain is. This place is right here and it's free, but, I don't know if you will like it. I hear that the action in the shower is pretty nonexistent," he laughed.

"Very funny, Greg. Just do your job...while you still have one."

"Yes, sir," he answered and slapped me on my ass.

EVER SINCE MEETING up with George, I came home in a good mood. We met two or three times a week, usually in the evening or the occasional Sunday morning. We would always meet in front of my house and run the exact same course. After several weeks, I felt myself getting stronger, and the run became like second nature to me. As we ran, we would talk about our jobs or the news and weather. We kept the subject matter platonic.

One day I arrived home and, as usual, the boys met me at the door with such enthusiasm that they almost knocked me down.

"Okay, okay. Let me change and we'll go out," I said, laughing at them,

My uniform at work consisted of a polo shirt with the logo of the spa on the left breast. I had a choice of either black or khaki slacks and comfortable shoes, or what I liked to call dyke shoes. It was easy enough to change into shorts and running shoes. I would take the dogs for a walk then, if I was lucky, maybe George would come by and we could go for a run this evening. Since I had started running, I was a regular client of Greg's, seeing him at least twice a week.

The boys had to urinate on everything. Even though they had been on this path many times, they seemed to be experiencing lots of new smells. We came up the street and as we were passing George's house, I looked over to see if there was any action. I hoped that I was not going to be a stalker in my old age. I noticed a white sedan coming down the street towards the dogs and me. I pulled the boys up on the lawn to let the car pass when it came to a stop and the passenger window went down.

"Chick!" It was George. "Do you want to go for a run?"

"Sure. I was kind of waiting for you," I shrugged.

"That's nice. Let me put my stuff down and change, I will be right up. By the way, great dogs!"

"Thanks." I forgot that I never introduced the boys to George. I pointed to the older dog. "This is Thom, and that one peeing on your shrub is Jerry. I needed to give them some quality time. See you soon."

In no time at all, George was out in front of the house. I could tell he was full of pent up energy. He was running in place until I came outside. He again had on black spandex shorts, running shoes, and a black sports watch.

"You ready?" he asked.

"Sure," I said and off we went.

Just like the times before, we ran to the beach. Once we hit the hard packed beach, we turned left and ran as hard as we could for six blocks. Four weeks ago, I would have been completely out of breath but this time I even beat George to the end of the packed sand. He smiled and slapped me on the back. We walked across the highway but jogged the rest of the way home easily. What used to take thirty minutes now took only twenty-two minutes from start to finish.

October

THE WEEK BEFORE Halloween the weather changed. The rainy season of summer was gone. So was the heat and the humidity. It was replaced with beautiful, sunny blue skies during the day and cool, dry nights filled with stars. I even opened my windows for the first time in two years. The dogs had their noses glued to the screen, hoping to catch a smell of someone walking by so they could bark a friendly hello to them.

Halloween used to be such an important holiday for both Eddie and me. We would decorate the house and dress up just to hand out candy to the kids in the neighborhood. I knew that there were some old costumes in a box high on a shelf in the garage. I could not venture into the garage just yet, so I went to the local party store and picked out some costume pieces. I chose a crushed pirate hat, an antique looking clip-on hoop earring, and a red bandana to wear as a scarf.

On Halloween night, I put on a black t-shirt and jeans. With inexpensive makeup that I purchased from the drug store, I painted on a moustache and a scar. I clipped on the earring, tied the bandana around my head and placed the hat on top of the bandana. I looked in the mirror and was pleased with the outcome. The doorbell rang and the first group of kids arrived as the dogs scrambled to the door.

When I opened the door, I was amazed at the group of five kids. They were between the ages of three and twelve. The bigger ones pushed through to the front.

"Trick or Treat," they chimed in unison.

I handed candy out to a skeleton, a clown, and someone dressed in a *Scream* costume with a black cloak and hood. They thanked me quickly and turned on their heels. They had many houses to go to before they were finished for the night and seemed eager for more candy. The two smaller children were left standing with their mouths wide open. My heart was full watching them stare up at me.

I kneeled down to their level, the bowl of candy in front of me. "What do you say?" I asked.

All they could do is stare with their mouths open.

"You've been practicing all day, honey. What do you say when you want candy?" one of the mothers coached from the foot of the steps.

"Here," I encouraged, moving in closer. "Just whisper it in my ear, okay?"

They nodded but said nothing.

"Come on," I said. "I promise I won't bite."

One took a big swallow and whispered, "Trick or treat?" making it sound more like a question.

"Are you going to say it too?" I asked the other. All I could get out of that one was a quick nod. "Good enough for me. Candy for all!"

I received smiles from both of them as they left.

"What do you say to the nice pirate?" one mother asked.

"Thank you," the two sang at the same time.

The smile was wiped clean off my face when the next child stepped onto my porch.

"What are you supposed to be?" asked a blonde-haired girl who was dressed like a green fairy.

"I could ask you the same question, young lady."

She stood there with one hand on her hip and sighed aloud.

"I am a pirate and I should make you walk the plank for such a question," I answered back.

"Just give me the candy, mister, so I can finish the rest of the neighborhood. Okay?"

"Blake, dear don't be so rude to the man," said a woman from the street. I assumed it was her mother.

"I'm sorry," Blake whined.

I tossed some candy in her bag, stepped back into the house and closed the door. I leaned my back against the door and took a deep breath.

"This," I said to myself, "is going to be a long night."

The knock on the door almost sent me to the hospital with a heart attack. I think I may have let out a little scream for the dogs came running to the door.

"Hold on, boys," I said to the dogs. "Let's not take a leg off some kid just because they are nasty."

When I opened the door, I saw two dark haired boys between the ages of five and seven. Obviously, they were brothers because they were the spitting image of one another. One was taller and I assumed he was the oldest of the pair, but they both sported the same crew cut. They were dressed in white karate kimonos and pants called a gi. The taller boy wore a yellow obi tied tightly around his waist, the other wore a white one. Black eye masks finished off each costume.

"And what are you boys supposed to be?"

"We're Ninja spies," they both shouted proudly. The little one was missing most of his front teeth. When he spoke, it sounded more like *thpieth.*

"I'm the Ninja master, and he's the student," the taller one informed me, pinching his brother.

"No, I am not," the smaller one shot back. He punched his brother in the arm.

"Ow," the taller one moaned, rubbing his arm and looking over his shoulder. "Dad, did you see that?"

I noticed that a handsome couple was standing in the shadows at the end of the driveway. They were dressed like Zorro and his wife, Elena. He was dressed entirely in black with a black eye mask, cape, and hat. Her dress was long, full, and red. She too wore a black cape and eye mask. Her dark curly hair was pinned up with soft tendrils cascading down her neck. The sight of them astounded me.

"Yes, I did. Now apologize to your brother." His voice was deep and familiar.

"I'm thorry," the smaller boy said in a whisper, his head down.

I kneeled down to his eye level, my big bowl of candy in my arms.

"That's okay. I'm a little brother too." I whispered in his ear. "But I got even."

"Oh yeah? How?"

"I grew taller and bigger than them. So I scared them."

He laughed.

I threw candy in their bags, making sure that the smaller one received more.

"Hey, that's not fair!" the taller one cried.

"I'm sure your parents are going to have you boys split the goodies evenly," I said waving to the couple as the boys scampered off the front porch. They both waved back. I had the feeling that I knew the man from somewhere but could not put my finger on it. I stood there watching the four of them disappear into the night.

November

"WHAT ARE YOU doing on Sunday?" George asked one

Friday while we were finishing our run.

"Nothing, I don't have any plans," I said panting for air.

"Now you do. I'm having a barbeque, and I have some people I want you to meet."

"What time?" I bent at the waist and put my hands on my knees. I did this to keep my knees from shaking with excitement and with any luck, it simply looked like I needed to catch my breath.

"How about two?"

"Great!" Now I did sound excited.

I felt like I was going on a first date. I changed my clothes six or seven times. I settled on khaki cargo shorts, a blue v-neck shirt and white converse slip-ons. I looked in the mirror.

"Not bad for an old guy," I told my reflection.

"What do you guys think?" I asked the dogs. They answered my question by wagging their tails.

"I'll take that as a yes."

I looked at the clock, and it was already after two. I took one more look in the mirror and thought that maybe I should have had Scott give me a quick trim on Saturday. I realized that would have been silly because he never would have had the time. He would have had his hands full with all those *tits on a stick* that he loves so much. I liked the way he cut my hair, but the thought of a straight hairdresser just did not seem right to me.

I walked to the fridge and grabbed the bottle of wine that I had purchased just for George's barbeque, said good-bye to the boys, and went out the front door.

THE LAST TIME I was preparing for a date I had clothes all over the bedroom floor because I did not know what to wear. I was going to meet Ed for our first official date. The night that I met Ed, both of us had too much to drink and ended up on a sleeper sofa at Herb's house. Herb was an old friend from high school. The sofa had belonged to my mother, and Herb took it so that I could have a place to crash when I was in the city. I lived across the bridge in Alexandria and the Virginia police were not too friendly to anyone caught drinking and driving. When Ed found out that Herb and his friend Denis were right around the corner with no door between us, he became so embarrassed and angry that I thought that he would never speak to me again.

I was twenty-six years old and had not yet started to go gray. In fact, I still had blond hair. It was not as bright as when I was a child. Suzanne, a stylist at the salon and a good friend, decided that I needed some enhancement, so she had placed some foil hi-lights in my hair.

"Cool," was all she needed to say.

With my bright blue over-dyed jeans and tight yellow t-shirt, I agreed. I do not need to say that I probably had on jazz shoes too, because it was the eighties. I did look cool.

I drove into the city and found the perfect place to park. I walked the three and half blocks to the restaurant.

Le Petit Café, a French restaurant, was in a part of town known as Adams-Morgan. The area got its name from combining two diverse schools; the first being an all black school called Thomas P. Morgan Elementary School and the second, an all white school named after the second president, John Quincy Adams. Now the neighborhood is home to many different ethnic cultures, especially Latin and Haitian, and has a hell of a block party at the end of the summer. We jokingly referred to it as *Madam's Organ*.

The restaurant was small and since it was Saturday night, it was cramped and loud. I walked in the door and instantly regretted what I had chosen to wear for the evening because everyone stopped what he or she were doing and turned around to look at me. I think the music may have stopped. I tried to spot Ed in the crowd

"Can I help you?" The man at a podium hissed. He was about my age. He wore his thinning, dyed black hair slicked back and flipped up at the collar. He had large dark eyes and a very wide mouth with full lips and too many teeth that gave him the look of a piranha.

"I'm looking for someone," I announced.

"Aren't we all," he sniffed.

Ed stood up over at the bar and waved. At six feet four inches tall, he was hard to miss. He had a head full of curly dark hair and a thick moustache. The design on his sweater matched my jeans perfectly as if we had planned it. His black jeans hung off his slim hips. When I finally reached him at the bar, he grabbed me and kissed me full on the mouth.

"Did you have any trouble parking?" he asked.

"Not really. I'm just down the street," I shrugged.

"What are you drinking?"

"Ah, whatever you are, I guess."

"Van," Ed boomed to the bartender, "Get my friend here an Absolut sea breeze." I learned that was Absolut vodka, with both cranberry and grapefruit juice.

He gave me the barstool that he was sitting on. Coming up behind me, he put his big hands on my shoulders. He introduced me to all the people around us. Ed had been sitting there for a while and had become quite chummy with the regulars at the bar. The bartender was a good friend of his and even though it was not happy hour, Van was giving Ed two or three drinks for the price of one. Everyone had heard all about me because Ed could not stop talking about me. They wanted to know where I worked and what I thought of their haircut. When they found out that I was also a massage therapist, they showed or told me all their aches and sore muscles. I was relieved, in some weird way, when the person with too many teeth showed up and whispered something in Ed's ear. Eddie grabbed him and turned him around to face me.

"Chick, I want you to meet my friend, Billy," Ed said to me. "Now Billy Dee, you be nice. I just met Chick last Saturday night."

A big broad smile grew slowly across Billy's face. It made him look like the Cheshire cat from Alice in Wonderland. His icy smile matched the coldness of his handshake.

"Oh, so you're the one from Saturday night," Billy said, his teeth gleaming in the bar light.

"What do you mean?" I could feel the blood rushing to my face.

"Oh, nothing," he oozed. He turned to Ed and whispered, loud enough for me to hear, "I thought you weren't going to see him again."

"That is not what I said," Ed whispered aloud between clenched teeth, his face showing no emotion. "I told you to be nice. Now, do you have a table for us or not?"

The piranha turned on his heel, large menus pressed up against him like a shield. "Right this way," he hissed.

Billy sat us in his section, which was up in the front of the restaurant by these huge picture windows. The table was small and our knees pressed together. We ordered our meal and let Billy choose the wine. I could not tell you what we ate or how the wine tasted because we were more interested in one another than the food and drink. Ed told me he grew up on Miami Beach.

"Have you ever been to Miami?" he asked.

"I passed through Miami once on my way to Key West," I replied.

"What did you think?"

"I loved it, but my friend Alice told me to stay away from the Cubans there."

"Oh, yeah," he said as a giant smile spread across his face. He leaned in real close and looked me in the eye. "You may have avoided them in Key West but not here in D.C.," he said with a laugh.

"I'm so sorry," I gasped. "I didn't mean that the way it sounded," I said, the blood rushing to my face. "It was the time of the Mariel Boat Lift and there were a lot of seedy people lurking about."

I was so embarrassed when I realized what I had just babbled. "I should just keep my mouth shut and take my foot out, right?"

He put his hand on mine to quiet me.

"That didn't bother me. In fact, I thought it was kind of cute."

I knew at that moment I had fallen in love with the man across the table from me. He was charming and attentive. I could picture us spending the rest of our lives together but for tonight, I could see the two of us tangled in the bed sheets. I smiled.

"Now why are you smiling?" he asked.

"Now, I really am embarrassed," I mumbled.

"What?"

"You will think I'm horrible," I blushed.

"I have to know. Why do you have that devilish smile?"

"I was thinking how good your sweater and my pants would look thrown over the back of a chair."

WALKING UP THE driveway, I noticed a faded bumper sticker for George W Bush on the back of a minivan. I thought to myself that this is going to be a very interesting party. I could hear Latin music playing and children laughing. I hesitated slightly then knocked on the door. In a short while, a tall, beautiful woman with dark eyes and wild curly hair opened the door.

"I'm...ah... Chick," I stuttered.

"So you are the Chick that I've been hearing about." She held out her hand and said, "I'm George's wife, Isabelle. Everyone calls me Bella."

I was beginning to feel like the lyrics to the song, "Ironic," by Alanis Morrissette. *You meet the man of your dreams and then his beautiful wife.*

I must have just stood there with my mouth wide open so Bella added, "Why don't you come in?"

George came to the door just in time.

"You can always count on the gringos to be early," he laughed, even though it was almost three o'clock. "I'm glad you came early. I see you've met my wife, Bella."

"Sure did. Just now. You are very beautiful," I choked out.

"Well, I can see that you and I are going to be good friends," she cooed, taking my arm and leading me into the house.

I handed Bella the wine.

"Oh, it's cold. Do you want me to open it for you?" she asked.

"No. Why don't you save it for a special occasion," I replied. The special occasion that I thought was supposed to be for George and me.

"Thanks, that's so sweet." She kissed me on the cheek.

The day was magnificent. The hot sun was shining and there wasn't a cloud in the sky.

Their backyard was wide but short, and the patio ran the entire length of the pool. The house on one side with large square pillars on the other supported a slatted arbor. Between each pillar were hanging baskets filled with flowering plants of many different types.

Even though it was Veteran's Day weekend, the long, rectangular pool had three kids splashing around in the shallow end. I recognized the blonde girl, Stella. She and her parents, Yves and Tina, lived across the street from me. They were from Switzerland. Yves worked for a software company, and Tina was an artist. I saw them both sitting at a table under a mango tree that was months away from being in full bloom. I waved and they waved back. Tina was wearing a bikini top and a brightly colored sarong tied at her waist. She had on a large straw hat and big white sunglasses.

I noticed that everyone was wearing some kind of bathing suit. George was wearing black trunks with a white stripe down the side. His Hawaiian print shirt was completely unbuttoned, showing off his hairless chest.

"I hope you don't mind getting your clothes wet," George said as though reading my mind, "because everybody's going into the pool." He handed me a beer.

"A few more of these, and you won't get me out," I laughed.

"Good," George agreed and we clinked bottles.

"You have a beautiful yard," I observed.

"Thank you, but I can't take the credit. Bella does all the work around here."

I looked over at the kids playing in the pool and said, "I know Stella, but who are the two boys?"

"They are my boys," he said proudly. "Juan is the oldest. He'll be seven at the end of June, and the one getting ready to cannonball is Aaron." Aaron jumped into the pool and for such a little boy, he displaced a lot of water.

"Aaron, like in Hank Aaron?" I asked.

"Yeah, how did you know? You like baseball?" George asked.

"My father was a ballplayer long before I was born and we watched it every Saturday afternoon on TV during season. In fact, he took me to the last Senators game at RFK stadium when I was a teenager. They were handing out plastic batting caps that day too. I have Marlins' season tickets. Would you and your boys like to come with me to a game or two?"

"That would be great," he said. We touched our bottles

together again to seal the deal.

C.P.T. stands for Cuban People Time. I was told to be at the house at two but most guests did not even begin to arrive until three thirty or four o'clock. The music was turned up a little louder then and the guests became more animated. It felt great to be around so many lively people and their families again. George introduced me to everyone as his new running amigo. I was having a hard time trying to understand their broken English, so I just smiled a lot and nodded my head.

After a few beers, I did find myself in the pool. With my wallet and keys safely tucked into my shoe, I dived into the deep end. I had forgotten how much fun kids were in the pool. I was the youngest in my family, and I grew up feeling that my nieces and nephews were more like my little sisters and brothers. They now have children of their own.

Juan and Aaron were like little carbon copies of George, from the color of their tan skin to their close-cropped haircut. Like most boys, they loved to be thrown up into the air to splash back into the water. I thought to myself that if I was going to be hanging out with these youngsters, I needed to stay in shape because they were making me tired.

The boys finally calmed down and let me relax on an inflatable raft as they hung on to my arms. George jumping into the pool, cannonball style, right by our heads, interrupted us. The boys and I attacked him, pushing his head under the water, laughing.

"You know my boys usually don't take to people as fast as they have to you," George said later. He was sitting on the pool edge with his feet in the water. I was in the pool with my head on my arms leaning on the pool deck.

"I do have a way with kids," I sighed.

"Didn't you want any?" he asked.

"I did but it wasn't in the stars for me."

"Were you ever married?" I'd been asked the question a thousand times. "I see you wear a ring."

"I was with someone for a long time," I said looking down at my ring. I felt that pang of emptiness in the pit of my stomach. It was time to come clean. I had had enough to drink and George seemed sincere with his questions, "He died."

"AIDS?"

"No, not AIDS." I hated people assuming that, but George seemed nonjudgmental. "Something much more typical; congestive heart failure. Looks like when he was a kid he had some illness like scarlet fever that weakened his heart. By the time he had it checked out, it was too late."

"I'm sorry."

"Yeah, me too. We were supposed to grow old together..." I looked at George. "Does this bother you?

"What?"

"That I'm gay."

"Hell no." He didn't hesitate. "In fact, half of the Dade County Fire Department is gay."

MONDAY MORNING CAME very early. The boys were still sleeping on their beds when I came out into the den.

"Come on lazy bones. Time to get up and go outside," I ordered.

Yawning and with squinting eyes, they reluctantly went out the back door. I smelled the coffee and went into the kitchen.

This day was going to be my first day back to the gym. Greg had reminded me how wonderful the facility was at the spa, and I was going to check it out. The only time I had been through the gym was on my initial orientation and I remembered it being not too big but clean. I had my uniform ready and I had even found my old gym bag.

It was still black outside when I was putting my gear in the back of my car. The sun would not be out for at least another hour. I heard someone jogging up the street.

"Where are you going so early in the morning?" It was George.

"I could ask you the same question," I shot back. "I'm heading over to the spa to work out at the gym there."

"That's cool. I'm going to Dale's new gym up next to the grocery store."

"When did somebody open a place there?" I asked.

"A couple of weeks ago. Hey, you want to come with me?"

"He's open at this hour?"

George showed me a key hanging from a chain and he started swinging it around his finger.

"No," he smirked, "but I sleep with the new aerobics instructor and she gave me the key."

"Ok, let me get a towel," I said.

"No need because Dale has thought of everything."

I slammed the back door of my car and off we went.

On the way, George told me that Dale, who owned the gym, had worked with Isabelle at another place. When Dale told Bella that he was going to open his own place, he asked her if she wanted to supervise the aerobics department and she said yes. When we arrived through the parking lot, the building was dark. George put the key in the lock and opened the door. He turned on the lights and turned off the alarm.

"Ready," he said. "Let me take you on a quick tour."

The first room was mirrored on all four walls.

"This is the aerobics slash spinning slash yoga room," George said with his arms outstretched.

Eight spinning bikes were lined along the back wall as well as some step equipment and a small stereo with speakers in the room. It seemed eerie not to hear music playing. Also, the air conditioning was not on, and the room suddenly felt very stuffy.

As if reading my mind George said, "God, it's hot in here. Let me turn on the AC."

He walked through a doorway at the other end of the room, flipped the switch, and the next room was filled with light. I heard the air conditioner come to life and figured that George had found the thermostat. I looked in the adjoining weight room. It was small, but the equipment was sufficient.

"Hey, Chick, come over here," George motioned me over. "Check this out."

He was standing in the locker room. I walked in and was pleasantly surprised because for such a small place, it was decorated handsomely. The floors were Italian tile, and the wooden lockers looked like pecan. At the end of the room were two tiled stall showers. They had large copper rain showers that poured down from the ceiling. In each shower were dispensers of shampoo, conditioner, and body wash. I made a note to myself that if I were going to be a regular at Dale's gym, I was going to have to upgrade the products.

"You're right. He does think of everything," I observed.

"He even has towels and stuff to shave with. I think you would like him," George added as he threw me a towel.

There was something strange about being alone in an empty gym with another man. It felt like one of those old seventies porno movies where the guys workout for two minutes and then get it on for the rest of the movie. I thought to myself that this was no time to be turned on even as I felt the erection rise in my shorts. I placed the towel in front of me. I know that George had turned the air on, but why did it suddenly feel so hot in the room?

"You okay?" he asked.

"Yeah... Hey, how about some music?"

Later, locking up after working out, George asked, "Well, what did you think? You like it here?"

"Yeah, sure," I commented. "Is the owner okay with us being here this early?"

"Sure. Dale is a great guy. You'd like him."

"You said that before."

"I did? Well, I think you guys would have a lot in common."

Thanksgiving is the official beginning of the winter season. This is the time when snowbirds flock down from the cold North and descend on sunny, south Florida. There was a time that the season began earlier, like the end of October or around the Jewish High Holy Days of Yom Kippur and Rosh Hashanah. Blame it on global warming or that the state of Florida will tax you for the year if you live in the state for six months.

The White Party at Villa Vizcaya is perhaps the most elegant of all charity functions; in fact, it is called the crown jewel of AIDS fundraisers. The Sunday after Thanksgiving, the mansion and gardens of farm equipment pioneer, James Deering, are transformed into a sparkling cavalcade of small, twinkling lights and beautiful people dressed entirely in white. One would almost feel as if he had walked into a chapter of *The Great Gatsby* were it not for the pounding techno beat radiating from the dance floor. It is truly a spectacle to behold. The week preceding, the affair is filled with lots of parties and festivities. Hotels are filled to the brim with wealthy gay patrons and their guests.

The Spa was not going to be outdone, and a grand opening party was scheduled for the Friday after Thanksgiving. The owners spared no expense in decorating the building, from the expansive floral arrangements in the lobby to the smallest details in the condominiums. People paid in excess of a million dollars to own their private space in a world-renowned spa and resort. Each room is furnished with state of the art television screens that can be used, with the help of a keyboard, like a computer. Guests can make reservations for one of the three restaurants or book an appointment for the spa or have a service enjoyed in the privacy of their own spacious apartment.

Ric stood at five feet seven inches and weighed a solid one hundred and seventy pounds. When he removed his bathrobe to lie down on the massage table, I was pleasantly shocked. At sixty-five years old Ric, or as I called him, Mr. B, carried no visible body fat. His tight lean frame was covered in a thick pelt of white hair.

"Mr. B, you are in great shape," I said covering the lower portion of his body with the sheet.

"Chick, if you don't mind, lose the sheet. I am not shy and besides, it's just you, me and Buck," Ric said, his voice muffled by the face cradle at the end of the bed.

Buck was Ric's partner and although he too had a head of silver hair, he was twenty years younger than Ric. I did what I was told and removed the sheet. I was envious of his tight butt.

Ric and Buck shared a home in Beverly Hills. They also owned a ranch in Palm Springs as well as a chalet in southern France. Buck kept a small apartment in Manhattan. Now they owned one of the six penthouse suites at The Spa. The two bedroom, two bath oasis on the thirty-ninth floor had the most beautiful view of the ocean and South Beach. The furnishings were minimal. Low white sofas faced the water and a glass dining table with eight matching chairs sat on the pastel-colored travertine tile that ran throughout the entire twenty-seven-hundred square feet. It was the perfect setting for a grand party.

I set up the portable massage table in the living area facing the ocean. As I massaged Ric's strong back, I looked out onto the horizon. A cruise ship, tiny on the vast ocean, was sailing for ports south. Everything was right with the world.

Buck passed by on his way from the bedroom to the kitchen. I turned from daydreaming to watch him walk past me. He too had a nice physique; flat stomach, broad shoulders that tapered to slim hips and like Ric, thick muscular legs. A small gray moustache was the only body hair I saw. He would be on the table soon, and I would find out for myself.

Ric moaned as I massaged the back of his legs. Buck caught my eye and winked; a sly smile crept over his face. I blushed.

"Mr. B, are you ready to flip over?" I whispered.

"Yeah, sure," he replied in a sleepy voice.

I helped him onto his back. Ric's erection stood straight up, resembling the mast on a sailboat. I was always a little nervous when things like this happened at work, especially when they happened in the guest's private quarters. I closed my eyes and took a deep breath. I was a professional, and I was going to get through with this massage. When I opened my eyes, Ric was staring up at me.

"Anything wrong?" he asked.

"Um, no, no," I mumbled.

"Don't pay that any attention, Chick. It has a mind of its own," he said with a hearty laugh. Instantly Ric's comment put me at ease. I finished the massage without hesitation.

"Chick, that was great!" he said, sitting up.

"Thanks," I answered.

"No, I mean it. It was probably the best massage I have ever received without a happy ending," he said with a wink. "What are you doing this evening?"

"I have no real plans."

"Aren't you married or something? You wear a ring."

"I was," I said, holding my hand up and looking at my gold band. "For more than twenty years."

"And what happened?"

"He passed away two years ago from a heart attack. In fact, April would have been our silver anniversary."

"I'm sorry," Ric offered, touching my hand.

"Thank you, Mr. B, but there is no need to be sorry. You didn't know."

"I want you to come to a little party that Buck and I are hosting here tonight. Now that I know you are single, it is imperative that you attend. You are single, aren't you?"

"Yes. Yes, I am very single." I said, my chin to my chest.

Ric stood up from the massage table and lifted my chin as he looked me in the eye.

"You're coming. That's all there is to say about that."

"I would love to, Mr. B, but the management doesn't like for the staff to fraternize with the guests."

"Nonsense, Chick, you are now our friend. I'll not hear another word about it! Be here at eight."

Ric threw his robe over his shoulder and walked out of the room, his firm buttocks moving side to side without a single jiggle.

Buck hurried into the room. He stopped at the foot of the bed and dropped his shorts, removing any doubt I had concerning his body hair.

I AM NOT one for a lot of jewelry. I wear my gold ring. And, though I know it is not very fashionable anymore, my Uncle Raymond's watch which he had worn in World War II. It still works; all you have to do is set it and wind it. What I liked about the watch was that it still sported the original brown, crocodile leather band. I decided on wearing it as well as a long sleeve white shirt, untucked, and faded, boot cut jeans with ankle high boots. A cocktail of Jack Daniels and soda completed my outfit.

I forgot how much I enjoy watching gay men interact with one another. The gentle touch on a sleeve as they talk or once they find someone attractive, they caress the part of their body they think is sexy.

Ric was busy taking photographs of everyone at the party. He was arranging people in different groupings, and it seemed that everyone was having a good time being involved with the pictures. Though Ric was a prominent attorney in Los Angeles, his true love was photography. He even had several galleries showing his studies of male nudes as well as two books on men over the age of forty in all their glory.

"You all know Chick, don't you?" Ric said, throwing his arm over my shoulder. "He is the best massage therapist in all of South Florida."

"I wouldn't go that far, Mr. B," I said.

"I would," he returned. "Whenever you're in town, you should try him out, er, I mean, let him give you a massage."

Ric started to laugh, and the whole group laughed aloud. That was what I liked about Ric; he made everyone feel at ease. No wonder his portraits were so perfect; I'm sure his models never worried about anything.

Not everybody was enjoying himself, in fact I noticed one guy who was not having any fun at all. He seemed out of place. I had an eerie feeling that I knew him from somewhere. He was dressed in faded khaki pants and a long sleeve white t-shirt under a dark polo. I could tell by his pale complexion and the dark circles around his eyes that he did not get out in the sun much.

His hair was cut in a mohawk style with the sides shaved and the top and back left longer. It was dyed waitress black. By that, I mean that it was the color of shoe polish, and had no shine whatever. His earlobes stretched open big enough that you could insert a quarter.

Ric walked by and I grabbed him.

"Who is that guy in the corner?" I asked, gesturing with my head.

"You mean Angel?" Ric asked.

"Angel who?"

"Just Angel. He goes by one name, you know like, Madonna or Cher. He is an artist on the beach, and I love his work. Do you want to meet him? You better be warned he is a bit of a cliché"

"Cliché?" I asked.

"Yeah, you know the brooding artist. The tortured soul. Please, his father died and left him a windfall."

"Windfall?"

"A lot of money. You know, Chick, sometimes I think you really did fall off the turnip truck. His father was in the Cuban black market. He sold jewelry, televisions, cell phones, you know. He made lots of money. I mean mucho thousands of dollars. He died of a heart attack and left all his money to Angel. Come on, I'll introduce you."

Before I could protest, Ric grabbed my hand and whisked me toward Angel.

"Hey Angel, there's someone here who wants to meet you. This is my good friend and massage therapist, Chick. He works here at The Spa," Ric said as he left the two of us alone in an awkward silence.

I cleared my throat.

"Hello, Angel," I said extending my hand. "It's nice to meet you. Ric says that you do some great work"

Angel did not move from his chair but looked me in the eye.

"I see you are still drinking," he mumbled.

"Excuse me?" I asked. I could not believe my ears. "Do I know you?"

"You are still drinking." His eyes never left mine.

"What do you mean by that?" I looked from side to side, nervously.

"Nothing."

With a disgusted look, Angel rose from his seat and left the room. That is when I noticed the tattoo on his neck, a large red rose with a dagger running through it and drops of blood disappearing into his shirt. I could feel my heart beat in my throat. I stood there dumbfounded.

"Is everything okay?" It was Buck. "Chick, I'm talking to you. Is everything all right?" He shook me.

"Yeah, sure." I turned to Buck, as if in a dream. "Have you ever met someone and felt like you've met them before?"

"Well. Yeah. Sure...him?"

"Yes, Angel. I have a weird feeling about him, and I don't know why."

I looked at my drink, put it down on the nearest table, said my goodbyes, and left.

December

"IT FREAKED ME out," I told George weeks later.

We were running on the beach. The sun was beginning to set, and a light breeze was blowing off the ocean. We were the only people on the beach at this hour because the tourists had left for the day. I had not seen nor spoken to George since the party but both of us seemed to need a good, hard workout to sweat out our frustrations.

George, Bella and the boys had spent the Thanksgiving holiday with Bernice, Bella's mother, in Naples, a two and a half hour drive from our neighborhood. Being there frustrated George because he simply hated to be away from his house for very long.

"I would be too," George agreed. "That's all he said to you?"

"Yes. Then he just walked away. It was the tattoo on his neck that was familiar. Don't people in prison have tattoos on their necks?"

We had reached the far end of the beach.

"It seems to me that tattoos are popping up everywhere on everybody. I guess they're not just for hoodlums anymore."

He laughed and changed the subject. "Let's go back down the

other way and come back then we'll head home, okay?"

"You're on!" I exclaimed.

We turned to go back down the beach and had just started to run fast when George hit the ground.

"Holy shit!" he yelled out, holding onto his leg. I stopped and turned to see what was wrong. I saw George on the sand holding his leg in pain.

"George, what's wrong?"

"Pain. Back there," he said, pointing to the area between his hamstring and his butt cheek. Even in the fading light of day, I could see that he was experiencing a muscle spasm and a severe one at that.

"Roll over on your stomach," I ordered. "Quickly."

He did as he was told.

I slowly straightened out his leg as much as I could with my right arm. With my left hand, I lifted the leg of his shorts exposing his firm buttock.

"You will not like this," I said as I dug my thumb deep into the spasm.

"Holy crap!" He screamed in pain.

"Just breathe through it, George," I said.

Slowly, I could feel the tension beginning to release. "That's it. Just breathe and you'll feel better."

"Oh, yeah," he said. "I'm feeling better already. Thanks. Oh yeah, that feels great." I was enjoying holding on to his muscular thigh so I started to massage his ass.

I heard someone behind me clear his or her throat. I slowly turned my head to see who it was. A police officer wearing a Town of Sea Breeze polo shirt and dark blue shorts was standing looking down at the two of us with his arms crossed in front of him.

"Umm. This is not what it looks like, Officer," I said. I could feel the heat rising in my face.

George looked up at the cop.

"Oh, shit," he said and put his face back into the sand.

"Why don't you tell me what you boys are up to, then," the officer said. His tone implied that he was not going to believe a word that we said.

"We were running," I started, "when my friend, here, developed a Charlie horse in his upper thigh, and I was applying direct pressure to the afflicted muscle."

"Hmm," the policeman grunted.

"Really, Officer," I pleaded looking at his name tag, Samuel Davis. "Officer Davis, I am a massage therapist at The Spa on Miami Beach. I know this looks funny but I promise you we are not up to anything. As you can see, my friend here is in serious agony."

"Yeah," he snickered, "I heard him moaning from over there." He pointed to the water.

"Ay, Dios mio," George muttered under his breath. I pushed my thumb deeper into his muscle, and he screamed into the sand.

"You are not helping matters," I whispered loudly to George.

"What did you say?" Officer Davis was beginning to sound very perturbed.

"My friend here is being a bit of a smart alec. He won't give us any more trouble. Will you, George?" He shook his head in the sand. "That's better," I said to him.

I turned to the officer, "I know this looks bad."

"Yes, it does."

I looked at the scenario. Here I was kneeling between my friend's wide open legs looking like I had my thumb up his ass while he was moaning in the sand. I could just image what the policeman thought.

I let go of George's thigh and sat down on the sand. It started as a chuckle, then grew into hysterical laughing.

"You know, Officer Davis," I said trying to catch my breath, "I wouldn't blame you for wanting to throw us in jail. I can only imagine what you thought when you saw us. You were probably thinking *holy crap these guys are fucking on the beach!*"

George started to laugh. He raised up on one elbow and brushed the sand off his face. He looked at me and the two of us broke out into uncontrollable laughing. Tears were streaming from our eyes.

"I'm glad that you have the situation well in hand," the policeman said smiling. That is when I knew that we were not going to jail for lewd and lascivious.

"I'm sure it looked pretty bad when you came up on us," I said, the laughter finally calming down.

"It was your friend's moaning that caught my attention. He's okay?"

"Yes sir and thanks. Thanks a lot."

"You bet. Have a great evening." With that, the officer turned and walked away.

THE CHRISTMAS SEASON had begun. When raised in the North, the thought of a warm holiday season just does not feel right. Nevertheless, after so many years of living on the beach, your views of Christmas change. I enjoy that I can open the windows and let the cool, salt air flow through the house. The dogs love having the opportunity of barking at everyone who walks by.

Call me Pollyanna, but I have a tendency to go overboard

during the holidays, especially this particular year. I had done nothing for so long that I almost forgot what I had out in the garage. I finally gathered my courage and opened the door to what I referred to as The Shrine. I had stored all of Ed's belongings in a dozen or so boxes, promising one day that I would do something with them.

Once out in the garage, I took one look at the pile of Ed's boxes and the sight astounded me. For an instant, I forgot why I had ventured out that way. I was out in the garage briefly at Halloween, but now I needed the courage to be there long enough to remove the Christmas decorations.

The Fat Boys is what I call my collection of Santas. They were always arranged on the buffet by the dining table. I was happy to see their smiling faces again. They had been hidden away in the garage with the other decorations for too long.

I dragged one of the boxes filled with tree ornaments out to the living room and after sitting down on the tile floor, I opened it up. Each ornament was wrapped carefully in colored tissue.

For us, Christmas ornaments had always been like a scrapbook that you open up every year, then adding new mementos to the collection. I removed one of the colored gifts from the box and with trembling fingers. I unwrapped it. For most of twenty years, I had repeated this scenario, and I listed in memory from where each and every ornament had come, tears slowly rolling down my face.

That night was the beginning of the nightmares. Dark slashes across my eyes. The occasional bright flashes of red... blood red. I felt eyes burning the back of my head. Something pressing all its weight on me, forcing my head down, almost suffocating me. I could feel pain all over my body. I would awaken frightened and disoriented. The one thing that kept reoccurring in my mind was the rose tattoo.

Angel, I thought. Why was he trespassing into my dreams? What was the connection between him and me? Each night as I slept, more and more of the story unfolded in my dream.

I walked into Angel's studio; his paintings were vivid and alive. When I talked to him, his eyes burned into mine. I was his slave. The rose tattoo on his neck was pierced with a gold dagger. Drops of blood were inked down the front of his chest, stopping on his soft, hairless stomach. He grabbed a handful of my hair and forced me to my knees. He shoved his huge, uncircumcised cock down my throat. The more he treated me like shit, the better I liked it. Forcing my face into the sofa cushion, he entered me from behind. The pain was intense, and I bit my lip to keep from crying out. Soon the pain turned into a sick pleasure. I remember reaching behind me to feel his body slamming into me. He slapped my hand away.

"Don't fucking touch me!" he shouted.

He grabbed a handful of my hair and forced my head up and back.

"You are mine," he sneered in my ear.

Our bodies were covered in sweat. He started to growl from deep in his throat like a lion as his rhythmic pounding became stronger. I could feel his orgasm start to boil up. He let go of my hair, and I let my head rest on the arm of the sofa. I matched his thrusts and soon we were both lost in the animalistic fever of sex.

"Fuck me harder!" I cried out.

"You like that, do you?" he asked, grinding his entire length in and out of me with all his weight. He forcibly pulled his cock out of my rectum and as he removed the condom, he shot his seed across my back. Both of us were out of breath. He placed his foot on my back and kicked me to the floor.

"Get out!"he cried.

This tableau would be repeated over a period of several weeks. I would leave work, go home, and down a few strong cocktails. Then I would find myself at Angel's studio.

I wanted to kiss him, but he refused. "No kissy-kissy," he would say.

I was hypnotized by the rose tattoo. He would force me to my knees as I unsnapped his pants and let them drop to the floor. I was mesmerized by his giant member. I loved to inhale his musky aroma. He would throw me down and violate me right on the dirty studio floor. He never let me touch myself. Sometimes I would ejaculate while he was breeding me, especially while he had me pressed to the ground. Leaving the studio, I always felt like trash and would go home and drink myself to sleep.

"Please God, help me," I would say as I fell into bed.

I remember the dark images with the vivid slashes of blood red, which were his paintings, and they frightened me. It was like looking at a train wreck, gruesome but fascinating. I could not get enough of Angel or his cock.

Once I was sitting at a local bar drinking excessively when my phone rang. It was Angel."Come here now," he said, then hung up.

I was loaded. The only good thing was that I could walk to the studio from the bar. I know that I reeked of vodka when I entered through the back door.

"Honey, I'm home," I said laughing.

Angel was standing there waiting for me. He was wearing cut off khaki shorts and converse tennis shoes. Both were covered with paint splashes. His arms were crossed across his bare chest. The rose tattoo seemed to be on fire, the drops of blood alive. I was afraid, yet enthralled. I walked over, threw my arms over his shoulders, and kissed him.

"You stink," he said pushing me away.

"Oh, come on, baby," I slurred. I pulled my shirttail out of my pants and unbuttoned it. "Just one little ol' kiss."

"You know that I don't like to kiss, especially when you stink like booze."

"You like it when I kiss your cock," I said as I reached out to unbutton his shorts. He slapped my hands away.

"You are drunk," he spit. "Stinking drunk and I want you out!"

I could feel the tears well up in my eyes. Telling me to leave hurt worse than him slapping me. I sank to my knees in front of him.

"Please, Angel, don't make me go. I love you."

He stood there glaring down at me.

"You love me?" he boomed. "You love... me?"

His voice became louder, and he started to laugh. "You think because I let you suck my cock that I show you any kind of love? Do you think that because I fuck you that I care about you? Look at you," he said placing his foot on my chest and pushing me down. "You are pathetic. Who would love you? You are no better than a drunk on the street, a filthy stinking bum on the street."

He unbuttoned his shorts and pulled down his zipper. He pulled his cock out.

"Yeah," I said. "That's what I want."

"You want this?" he laughed. "You want this?"

"Yeah, give it to me."

"I'll give it to you all right. Just like the street trash that you are." He began to urinate on me.

"Hey, what are you doing?" I cried out. "Stop!"

He placed his foot on my chest and held me down while he finished humiliating me.

"Now you really look and smell like a drunk on the street," he said. He spit in my face. "I'm going to throw your ass out into the street where you belong."

He grabbed the front of my shirt and pulled me up, almost ripping it off me. I burst into tears.

"Why are you doing this to me? What have I done? Why can't you love me like I love you?" I sobbed aloud.

"What do you know about love? How could anybody love a pathetic, stinking drunk like you?"

Each word was like a punch to my gut. He forced me up and pushed me toward the back door.

"Please, Angel," I pleaded. "Don't do this to me. I will be good. I will not drink any more. Just let me stay."

He flung open the door and threw me up against the building across the alley. While I was in Angel's studio, a steady rain had begun to fall and everything was wet. A small stream of water flowed down the middle of the alleyway.

"Get the fuck out of my sight! I never want to see you again."

He spit at me and slammed the door shut. From outside I could hear him lock the door. He turned the outside light off. It was dark and I was alone. I slid down the wall and sat on the wet pavement. I burst into uncontrolled sobbing.

I had loved someone and that person had loved me unconditionally. At one time in my life, I was complete, and now my life was in shambles. I was so lonely that I thought my heart was going to break. I leaned my head back on the wall and let the rain fall on my face.

I must have sat there for some time because I eventually noticed that I was soaking wet, and that my head was throbbing. I pulled myself up and headed for the only light I could see, a streetlight at the end of the alley. I could barely walk; my legs felt like rubber. When I reached the end of the alley, I was disoriented. I did not know where I parked my car.

"Come on, Chick. Don't be stupid. You've got to know where you left your car," I told myself. I headed up the street.

The images of Angel yelling at me and pissing on me kept flooding back. My head was swimming and my back was hurting.

By sheer luck, I found my car and waiting for me on the windshield was a parking ticket.

"Oh fuck!" I screamed toward heaven.

I reached into my pants pockets for my keys but they were gone. What was I going to do? I was too drunk to remember where I had left them. I could not go back to Angel's. Besides, I stank like booze and piss. My head was spinning while my stomach churned. Suddenly I fell to my knees in the gutter next to my car and threw up. I remember saying out loud, "Please God, help me!"

THE POUNDING ON the front door awakened me from the horrible nightmare of memory.

"God, you look like shit! What happened to you?" George exclaimed standing on my front porch.

I burst into tears.

"I remember everything about Angel," I said. We were sitting at the dining room table drinking coffee. It was our regular morning to run to Dale's gym and work out. George was concerned when I was not already awake and that, when he arrived, he had to pound on the door to rouse me. Even the dogs barking could not awaken me.

"It was horrible, George. The things I allowed him to do to me. Why was I so attracted to him? Why was I so fascinated?"

I told him everything. If he was embarrassed, he did not show it. George sat there quietly and listened to me ramble on. We had finished our second pot of coffee when the sun started to rise.

"Listen, I'm not gay, but I know why you were attracted to him. It's because he was dangerous and you were hurting from Ed's death. He is the total opposite of you; that hair and that shit he did to his ear lobes. Don't get me started on that tattoo either." He smiled."You have nothing to worry about now. That prick is out of your life and if I ever run into him, I will really fuck him over," George said, placing his arm over my shoulder. I laid my head on his arm.

"Thank you, George. What would I do without you?"

THAT WEEKEND GEORGE and his boys helped me pick out a tree and set it up in my living room. I insisted on the biggest one that George's SUV could carry. Bella, with the help of her mother Bernice, in from Naples for the holidays, fixed dinner, and the six of us listened to Christmas music and decorated the tree. We laughed and sang along with the likes of Frank Sinatra and Andy Williams. I've always said it's not Christmas until Nat King Cole sings "The Christmas Song."

Even the dogs got into the spirit by wearing their Santa hats and jingle bell collars. It felt so wonderful to have a house full of people enjoying themselves. The boys placed the unbreakable ornaments near the bottom of the tree, so the dogs would not hurt them. George pulled out the ladder from the garage and both of us hung the smaller, more delicate ones near the top. Bella and Bernice directed everything from the comfort of my sofa.

"Would you ladies like a glass of wine or anything?" I asked, flopping down on the sofa between Bella and her mother.

"No, thanks," Bella belched. "I haven't felt very well all day."

"I'm sorry. Anything I can do?" I asked sincerely.

"No dear, but it sucks to be sick at Christmas."

"What are you doing Christmas Eve?" George inquired.

"I really don't have any plans yet," I responded.

"Now you do," echoed George and Bella while at the same time exchanging smiles. There was even a tiny wink from George.

"George loves Christmas," Bella said. "Can't you tell?"

He was on the ladder hanging the wooden bead garland from

the top branches. He was leaning way out, and the muscles on his arms were straining. The weather was tropically warm, and George was wearing shorts and a tank top. A light mist of perspiration covered his chest. He was lost in what he was doing and it seemed the beads had to be hung just so. He strung and re-strung the beads several times before he thought them perfect. Finally, he realized that the conversation had ended, and we were all looking at him.

"What?" he asked, blushing.

"Hey, what's this? A pickle?" Aaron asked holding up a glass ornament.

"Yup," I said. "It's a tradition in Germany. Someone would hide a real pickle on the tree and whoever found it on Christmas day would have good luck all through the holiday. You found it so you get the good luck, big guy."

"We celebrate Christmas on Christmas Eve, and we call it *Noche Buena*. We get to stay up all night long and open presents and eat flan," he said.

"Daddy has a baby pig delivered with an apple in its mouth," Juan chimed in. "It's kind of gross, but it is so delicious. Yummy!" He grinned, rubbing his stomach and licking his lips.

We all laughed.

I took in the whole scene, sitting between Bella and Bernice, watching George and the boys decorate the tree, while the dogs followed the boys everywhere. I felt complete and heaved a long sigh of relief. Bella placed her hand over mine and put her head on my shoulder.

"With all of us around, you are never going to be alone, I promise," she whispered in my ear.

Tears started their way down my cheek. "As much as I've missed Ed, I am having such a great time today with all of you," I said thankfully.

"It's nice having you as a part of our family," Bernice said patting my knee and as if I had called him, Jerry came over and laid his head on my knee. His big brown eyes reminded me of Ed.

Christmas Eve finally arrived, and the weather could not have been more beautiful. The Spa closed early but before it did, the staff massed on the pool deck to wish one another a happy holiday. Since there were so many different nationalities employed at The Spa, we each shared our special traditions with one another. The tables were laden with all types of food and drink.

Greg and his guy friends were in a group at the far end of the pool. They were laughing and slapping one another on the shoulders. Greg looked up and gave me a small wave as to say *Happy Holidays*.

Same to you, my friend, I thought as I raised my glass of

champagne to him. I stayed out by the pool for just a short time. I needed to finish some paperwork and check the schedule for the next few days. Since it was the holidays, we were on a very quiet schedule with a minimal staff. I also wanted to get home to wrap my gifts for George and his family. I hoped that I could squeeze in a nap in before I got ready for *Noche Buena*.

WHEN ED AND I first moved to Miami, Ed had to work over the Christmas holiday. I wanted to spend time with his Cuban family and experience *Noche Buena* first hand. I had heard about the tradition for many years, but for some reason, Ed and I never celebrated it. Finally, we had the opportunity.

Awkwardly, I found myself to be the only person dressed for the occasion. Everyone else was in shorts or dressed very casually, with the exception of Eddie's mother, Aurora. Predictably, her hair was styled, and her makeup impeccably applied. I remember sitting on the beach one day with Aurora and her sister, Cuca. They were dolled up with their hair and makeup done perfectly, sitting glamorously under a large beach umbrella. Both women wore long sleeves and pants. Quite an unforgettable image.

The party was held at Ed's brother Albert's house. Albert was named after their father. Albert and his wife Patty have three children. The youngest is Jessica. At that time, she was just beginning to walk. Kris was ten, and Danice was twelve. Eddie's Uncle Raul and his wife Marta were there as well as Patty's mother and father from Santa Fe.

The house was small but clean. A three foot artificial Christmas tree stood on a short table next to the dining table. On the tree hung three letters addressed to Santa from the kids. For years, the tradition of letters to Santa would continue until all the kids became young adults.

The table was set with heavy paper plates, paper napkins and stainless eating utensils. Two bottles of red wine were open while an array of mismatched wine glasses and two glass candleholders-probably a wedding present-with white candles on top of a plastic, disposable Christmas tablecloth finished the tablescape.

"Dinner is ready," Patty had announced.

Like a herd of wild water buffalo, the family ran from their seats in the living room to their seats in the dining area, leaving me standing by myself with a glass of red wine in hand. I felt like the gringo outsider until Ed's father looked over at me and said in a thick Cuban accent, "Come here and sit next to me." He patted the folding chair next to him.

I was unaccustomed to this kind of behavior. Growing up my

family had a motto at dinnertime: Grab it and growl.

Why did I feel out of place? Could it be that it was my first time being with my partner's family, and I was the only adult not speaking Spanish? I squeezed between Eddie's father and Marta, who placed her hand on mine and gave me a sweet smile. I took a long sip from my wine glass. Suddenly, I felt much better.

Patty came to the table with a large pot and placed it on the table next to her father-in-law Albert. It was filled with steaming, white rice. Next, she emerged from the kitchen with another pot, this one filled with black beans. The aroma of garlic and onion filled the air. Ed's father, who was referred to as Papi, helped himself to an extra large serving of rice and as I observed, he made an indentation in the mound. This was, no doubt, for the coffee-mug-size portion of black beans he placed there. The steam rose from his plate like an active volcano. Though his plate was quite full, I wondered, how he could pile even more on it. Amazingly he did. I started to relax. Families aren't that different after all.

Noche Buena traditionally has a suckling pig as the main course. It was easier for Patty to serve a leg of pork instead. It was the size of a large turkey and had already been sliced. Patty had barely placed the heavy platter on the table when Papi grabbed his fork and speared two of the biggest slices of pork. Again, he showed me how much he could pile on his plate. Next to be consumed were the sweet, fried plantains and yucca with olive oil and garlic. It would not be complete without hot, fresh Cuban bread and butter.

Eddie had told me once that his father was six feet tall. Either that was a lie or he had shrunk considerably after sixty. The man beside me was barely five foot nine and weighed a whopping one hundred and thirty pounds soaking wet. A series of heart attacks had forced him to quit smoking cigars and to watch what he ate. Today was an exception.

I was surprised that after everyone was served, no one was going to say grace for this beautiful meal, one that I knew Patty had slaved over all morning long.

Papi had just begun devouring his meal when I cleared my throat and stood up, pushing my chair back with my legs.

"I would like to say grace," I said holding my hand out first to Papi, then to Marta, waiting for her to take my hand. She took my hand, then turned to her husband, Raul, and grasped his hand.

When all hands were clasped, I bowed my head.

"Our Father," I started. "who art in heaven..." I paused. Looking up, I glanced at Ed's mother. She was looking at me with eyes so filled with love that I almost forgot what I was doing.

"Por favor, Mami, ayudame," I said.

Still holding onto her granddaughter's hands she too stood.

"Santificado sea tu Nombre," she said out loud in a voice that quivered.

One by one everyone at the table rose to their feet. "Venga tu reino," the Cubans said in unison while I finished the Lord's Prayer in English. When we were done, I bent over and kissed Ed's father on the cheek. I turned and kissed Marta in the same respectful way. I winked at Aurora and she smiled back.

When we resumed our places, everyone dug into their plates. Not a word was said. I watched, with total amazement as Papi ate. How could a man so small and petite eat so much? He ate with much relish, not even stopping to drink any kind of beverage. He was like an eating machine, and when the last drop of black beans was sopped up with the last bite of bread, he stopped. From the top pocket of his shirt, he pulled out a toothpick and leaning back in his chair, he began extracting bits of dinner from between his teeth. Albert finished his meal about the same time as Raul.

Kris, who hardly ate anything, was the first to stand up and head to the living room. Everyone rose from the table and left me sitting there all by myself. I was so enthralled with watching Papi eat that I had barely touched my own food. With my napkin on my lap, I decided to finish my meal with or without company.

"Hey, Chick is still at the table," Patty said, laughing from the kitchen doorway. Everyone in the living room looked at me in the dining room and must have felt sorry for me because they left the game on the television and rejoined me at the table where they sat and stared at me until I finished eating.

IT WAS PITCH black outside when I woke up. I still had on my work uniform. I was disoriented and thought that I had overslept. I was relieved to see that I had plenty of time to get ready, it wasn't quite nine o'clock, and I was not going to be laughed at for being early this time.

The hot water from the shower felt good on my skin. I shampooed my hair and washed my face. I took the loofah to my entire body, especially my back, shoulders, and feet. When I emerged, I knew that my skin glowed.

With the fog blown off the mirrors with the aid of an old blow dryer, I looked at my reflection. My hair was mostly gray, even in my eyebrows and other places. In fact, when I saw my first gray pubic hair, I almost sat down and cried. The dark circles that once haunted me from under my eyes had finally faded away, and I didn't quite mind the not so tiny wrinkles. I stood sideways and looked at my body profile. Not bad, I thought, as I sucked in my stomach a little bit. Three months earlier, I had been mortified at my reflection in the mirror, but now I could honestly say I was pleased. With the help of George and our daily workouts, I had trimmed up and put on some muscle.

"Yes," I said to myself, "you might be a nice catch for someone."

In Miami, no one wears a tie anymore, not even to church. I picked out a pair of black, light wool dress pants, a pastel-pink button down shirt, and a gray sports coat. Red pocket square and black loafers completed my ensemble. I looked down at Jerry who was curled in a ball next to the dresser.

"What do you think, big boy?" I asked the dog.

Without lifting his head, he wagged his tail thumping it on the wooden floor.

"Where's your brother?"

Thom was out in the den. Lately, he seemed never to venture far from his bed. Approaching the room, I saw where one of the dogs had gotten sick. I kneeled down and stroked Thom. He rolled over so I could scratch his belly.

"You okay, buddy?" I asked.

I touched his nose, and it felt warm and dry. "Oh poor baby, you aren't feeling well."

I ran my hands over his muzzle. His hair used to be red, but now his face was mostly white. He seemed to fall asleep as I petted him.

I went into the kitchen for some cleaner and paper towels. The color of the sickness was a yellowish color, but it had no smell. I cleaned up the mess being careful not to get anything on me. Since Thom was snoring loudly, I knew he was asleep, and I could leave him alone and go to the party.

I tried to take my time, but I was still early. Just chalk it up to being a Virgo. I guess even when I die, they would never call me late. Bella answered the door wearing a red sweater over a white shirt and black slacks. Her crazy hair was pulled back in a tight bun. She wore no make up with exception of lip gloss. Her complexion was pale at best.

"Bella, you feeling all right?" I asked.

"No, not really," she answered.

"If I didn't know better, I would think that you were pregnant," I said with a laugh.

At that moment, George walked in the room. The sight of him dressed up made my heart skip a beat. He was wearing a traditional shirt from Cuba, a guayabera, white with long sleeves. Down the front on both sides was the most beautiful embroidery. It had one breast pocket and two pockets, one on each hip. Because the hem was cut straight around, the shirt was worn out over slacks. I had seen Ed's father wear them many times, but mostly his had short sleeves. George also wore tan slacks and brown loafers

"You clean up nice, man," I said. He did too, as the light shirt and slacks looked great against his naturally tan skin color.

"I do my best," he said with a nod in Bella's direction. I understood instantly that Bella picked out George's clothing.

"If it was up to him, he would wear those black swim shorts and that horrible Hawaiian print shirt." Bella said, her hands on her hips

"Now Bella, love of my life, don't make fun of my favorite party clothes," George said.

"If I didn't think you would kill me in my sleep, I would burn those silly threads."

The Christmas tree was placed perfectly in front of the floor to ceiling windows. It was a live tree. You could smell it the moment you walked into the house. It was decorated in white lights with gold and burgundy balls. There were clear glass snowflakes the size of grapefruits hung with silver ribbon. Around the base of the tree ran a small electric train. It looked as if it could have been in the window of Lord and Taylor in New York. I stooped over to place the gifts I had brought next to some other gifts under the tree.

"Your tree looks beautiful," I said sincerely. "Let me guess. George?"

"Yes," both George and Bella answered.

"I told you that he loves Christmas," Bella added.

"George, if you weren't spoken for, I would snatch you up in a minute," I said laughing.

"Sometimes I would let you have him," she answered back, a wicked smile on her lips.

I stood up as George walked over to me. He put his arm over my shoulders and slapped me on my chest.

"Damn, you are getting solid," he said reaching under my jacket and resting his hand on my chest. I am sure he could feel my heartbeat. It was almost jumping out of my body. He looked me in the eye, and I almost stopped breathing.

"Hey baby," he said turning to Bella. "Go see if the boys are ready, and grab the camera. I want a picture of me with our new friend in front of the tree. We are friends, right?"

"Right," I choked.

"My New Year's resolution," George said as soon as Bella was out of the room, "is for you and me to be better friends."

He raised his eyebrows and I was paralyzed. All I could do was stand there and look into his gray-green eyes searching to find the meaning behind his statement. It was the flash of the camera that brought me back to reality.

"Now I have a picture of my two, big men," Bella said with a laugh. Juan and Aaron ran into the room looking like little replicas of their father. Just like George, they too wore white guayaberas with long sleeves and tan slacks. They threw their arms around George and me.

"Now let me get a shot of all my men," Bella said.

The church was small, so space was at a minimum. Literally, every pew was filled. The church staff brought in folding chairs and placed them around by the walls. There was standing room only. George sat next to Bella and I was next to George. Juan sat on his father's lap, and Aaron sat on mine. The service had not yet begun, but I had already started to sweat with George's body heat next to me, and Aaron pressed up against me. I was relieved when I spotted Bernice looking for a seat.

"Bernice," I said standing up, "over here." I waved at her with Aaron on my hip.

"Listen, guys, I'm going to the back and stand up. Bella, your mom can have my seat. It is way too hot in here, and it has to be better toward the back." I handed Aaron to his father.

"Oh no, you don't. You're not getting away that easy," George said. "I'm going with you." He stood up.

Bernice worked her way down the pew while George and I went the other way. I turned around to see Bella's mother mouth *thank you*. I waved.

It was much cooler by the back wall. In addition, I had a better view of the inside of the church. It was beautifully decorated for the holiday. The electric overhead lights were dimmed, and candles were lit everywhere. There was a special section off to the right side where you could make a small donation and light a candle in someone's memory. If Ed was alive, he would have lit two candles, one for each of his parents.

I lit three.

The altar in front was decorated with red and white poinsettias with two tall candles burning on either side. On the back wall, small votive candles highlighted Jesus on the cross. On either side of the crucifix were two stained glass windows, one depicting the birth of Christ in a manger and the other, the borrowed tomb with the stone rolled back, Jesus ascending to heaven. Since it was almost midnight, both windows were lit with spotlights from the outside.

I would not consider myself a religious man, but when I see these images in stained glass, my heart is filled with love and compassion. I leaned up against the wall and let my head rest on the cool surface.

"You were right; it is much nicer here," George observed.

I could not have agreed more.

A small, white haired woman with wire-rimmed glasses and a dark blue choir robe entered the chapel from a side door. She held a folder of papers as she moved to the organ and sat down. She arranged the sheet music in front of her. Organ music filled the room. As she played, the choir of about twenty men and women filed into the room from the same door and took their places behind her. The last of the singers to enter was obviously the choral director for he stood facing them. He lifted his arms and led them in Handel's "Hallelujah Chorus."

"Hallelujah!" the choir sang triumphantly.

The hair on my body stood straight up.

"Hallelujah!"

Their voices were magnificent and as they sang, the processional of altar boys and girls with tall candlesticks entered followed by two priests. Their white robes were accented by burgundy and gold vestments. One priest was younger with thick black hair and a stocky build while the other was much older with a stooped posture. The older priest took a seat in a high-backed, velvet-covered chair. He was not seated for very long before his eyelids became droopy, and he slumped in the chair.

"Looks like Father Frizzell is up way past his bedtime," George said with some amusement. He pronounced the priest's name Friz-elle.

"How long has he been here?" I asked.

"Since the church was built, in the fifties," George whispered.

That would make him to be about eighty years old, and he looked every bit of that.

"Who's the other one?"

"Father Fuentes."

"Like Daisy?" I asked with a smile.

George laughed aloud with a snort, and people turned around to look. He turned bright red. "Yes, I guess so," he whispered.

Father Fuentes faced the congregation, and raised his hands, "Hallelujah! The Christ child is born this night in Bethlehem."

I could not understand a word he said. It came out sounding more like *Dee cry shile eez vorn dis nite een vet-la-ham*. Oh no, I thought to myself, Ricky Ricardo is performing Midnight Mass. Next would be the Babaloo chorus, I predicted.

I pulled George over to me and whispered in his ear, "I don't understand a single word he said."

"Don't worry, neither do I. I speak two languages, but I still don't understand either one of them. The best thing to do is just stay awake and enjoy the music. I love Christmas music."

I was not raised in the Catholic faith. The closest that I ever came was Mass at the Episcopal Church when I was a kid. I did not know the procedure, but we did receive a program that told us what would happen next. There were times when the priest spoke, and the congregation expected to answer back. At least the answers were written, and all I had to do was say them aloud. And like George, I also liked Christmas music and knew most of the words. When it was time to sing, I did not need a hymnal.

"Oh come all ye faithful, joyful and triumphant. Oh come ye, oh come ye to Bethlehem," I sang loudly and strongly. George looked at me and smiled. He joined in, "Come and behold Him, born the King of angels."

We were having so much fun singing that we didn't realize that the last two rows of people had stopped singing and were watching us. At least they had smiles on their faces. The young priest, Father Fuentes, walked down the aisles with a large guilt censor on a long chain. The smoke from the incense permeated the air. He was followed by the altar boys and girls, holding their candlesticks high in the air. With the organ music and the voices and the pageantry of the small church, one could not help but be affected. It was majestic and spectacular.

I started laughing after they passed by.

"What's so funny?" George asked, surprised at my sudden laughter.

"All I can think of is what Tallulah Bankhead said to the priest."

"What was that? I'm afraid to ask," George hesitated.

"Love your gown but your purse is on fire!"

We both burst out laughing. This time everyone turned to look at us, even Father Fuentes. That made us laugh even harder.

Father Fuentes, with the help of one of the altar boys was blessing the wine for communion. Holding his hands above a small, metal basin, Father Fuentes waited while an altar boy poured water over his hands. The boy passed the priest a small linen towel to wipe his hands. The wine was poured into a large, silver chalice which the priest held above his head for all to see. He placed the cup on the altar, then raised a small paper-thin wafer above his head, and broke it in half. He stepped to the front of the altar as people started to line up to take Holy Communion.

"Are you going up?" George asked me.

"I'm not Catholic," I answered back. "Are you?"

"No way. I'm afraid that I might spontaneously combust!"

The boys ran up to us when the service was over. With Juan in his father's arms and Aaron in mine, we maneuvered our way into the nave of the church. Standing at the front door was Father

Fuentes and Father Frizzell, the older priest who had slept during most of the service. To get out the front door we would have to bypass both men. As we walked to the exit, Father Fuentes held out his hand. George was the first to take it.

"Thank you Father, for a very memorable service," George said trying to be pleasant.

"So glad you boys enjoyed it," the priest said.

"Oh yes, we did a lot!" Juan exclaimed. "Now we can go home and open presents!"

We all laughed.

"Pardon mi, Jorge, quien es su amigo?" The priest asked George.

"I'm sorry, Father, this is my friend Chester," George answered respectively placing his free hand on my shoulder.

Father Fuentes offered me his hand, and I took it.

"Shester, it ees a pleasure to meet with ju," the priest said in his broken English, like a bad impersonation of Antonio Banderas. He firmly held on to my hand.

"Father, the pleasure is mine," I said.

"You can call me Joaquin," he said, still holding onto my hand. His accent was so thick I could barely understand him.

"Joaquin?" I asked, "as in Phoenix?"

"Yes," the priest answered, "I'm afraid so."

After dinner, we made ourselves comfortable. I had taken off my jacket and placed it on the back of the dining room chair. George took off his white shirt and replaced it with a Christmas t-shirt that said *Dear Santa, I want everything*.

Bella was still not feeling completely herself and had retired into a nightgown and a long, red satin robe. She said that the color made her feel a little more festive.

Bernice reminded me so much of Ed's mother. Especially by the way she usually dressed. It was something that I coined Middle age chic. Her outfit tonight had consisted of a dark green pantsuit, the jacket unbuttoned to show the green and red print top underneath. A red silk scarf had completed the look. Her red shoes had been removed hours ago and now she was wearing red pajamas with white piping down the legs. The boys, wearing matching cowboy pajamas that I had bought for them, were playing quietly on the floor in front of the tree. George's boys acted well behaved for youngsters who had been up all night.

Just as Juan had said, we were going to stay up all night and eat. The dinner was delivered by a company in Hialeah around three o'clock; a suckling pig, black beans, white rice, plantains, and Cuban bread. It was completely ready, and all we had to do was warm it up in the oven.

There was so much food. Between the six of us and the six guests we had invited, there were a total of twelve people. Therefore, George ordered enough food for twenty.

"I don't want anyone to go home hungry," he said.

No one did.

When the dishes were washed and dried, George and I flopped down on the sofa. Bernice, looking like a Christmas elf in her red pajamas, poured us both a glass of wine.

"Merry Christmas, George," I toasted.

"Merry Christmas to you, too, my friend," George answered back as we touched glasses, the sound of the crystal ringing throughout the room.

"Aaron, bring me those gifts for Uncle Chick, please," George instructed his son.

"You bet!" he exclaimed jumping up. Aaron picked up three brightly wrapped boxes and brought them over to me.

"Wow! All for me?" I asked.

"Yeah and we helped pick them out too," he said proudly.

"Well then, they will be all that much better."

I started with the smallest one. It was wrapped in green foil paper. I carefully peeled back the paper so as not to rip it, revealing a black box. Inside the box was a watch. Not just any watch, a running watch, just like the one that George wore.

"It's a Garmin Forerunner 405 GPS. It can tell you how far you've run, calories burned, and heartbeats per minute," George said with a smile. "It even vibrates so Bella likes it too."

"I do," she agreed laughing.

The second box was the biggest, and it contained a pair of running shoes. Once again they were just like George's, lightweight black with a bright red swoosh on the side. The last gift I had already guessed before I opened it. I was on the money; it was a pair of black spandex running shorts.

"I just hope you don't look better in them than I do," George chuckled.

"That will never happen because I don't have the Jennifer Lopez Latin booty that you have, George."

"Don't hate me because I'm beautiful," he said smiling. All of us laughed, even the boys, but I don't think they understood what we were talking about.

"My Christmas wish has already come true," I said with tears of joy in my eyes. "I have the family I've always wanted."

"That and you got the priest's home phone number," George said laughing.

January

EVER SINCE I moved to South Florida I have had a custom of diving into the ocean as my New Year's Day baptismal. This particular New Year 's Day was bright and sunny, without a cloud in the sky. I walked from my house to the beach, a large towel thrown over my shoulder. When I got to the beach, George was waiting for me at the water's edge.

"Are you sure you want to do this?" he said shivering.

"I do it every year. It's my thing," I chuckled. "One year it was so cold I thought that my balls would never come back down."

"If you can do it, so can I."

"Let's go!" I dropped my towel in the sand, peeled off my shirt, kicked off my sandals, and both of us ran to the water. Once our feet touched the water, we both stopped.

"Well, go on," George urged.

"I will. I will, don't rush me." I took a deep breath, faced east, and dove into the waves. The cold water took my breath away. I jumped up and out of the water, turning to face George, who was still standing in the shallow water.

"Come on, sissy boy, the water is fine." My voice was high pitched.

George screamed like a woman and ran into the waves. When he emerged from the water, his eyes were wide open. "Holy shit!" he exclaimed.

"Great, huh?" I asked, laughing.

"You owe me a pair of balls," George barked as he jumped on me and pushed my head under the water.

As we walked home, both of us thawed out under the bright sun.

"I hate to admit it, but that felt great. I feel like a new person," George agreed.

"Told you."

No New Year's Day is complete without ham, black-eyed peas and collard greens. The night before, I had been with George and his family watching Dick Clark ring in the New Year. At midnight, we toasted with champagne, and everyone kissed. It was very natural to kiss George on the lips.

"Yes," I had whispered in his ear, "we are good friends."

Now the family was coming to my house. I had the spiral cut ham in the oven, the greens were steaming, and the black-eyed peas were warming on the stovetop. I was plopped on the sofa watching *The Twilight Zone* marathon on The Sci-Fi Channel when the doorbell rang. It was George and his boys.

"Where is Bella?" I asked.

"She is still not feeling well so the women are just going to lay low," George said. "Oh look, boys, *The Twilight Zone*. I used to watch this when I was your age," he gestured toward the television as he took my place on the sofa.

"I'm sorry that they aren't here. I have a special treat," I hinted.

"What am I, *arroz con leche*?" George asked.

"No, of course not. You know what I mean."

George rose and walked into the kitchen. "Where's your treat?" he asked.

Oh, if you only knew, I thought to myself.

On the counter was a sterling silver punch bowl filled with a southern delight, milk punch. My recipe was very different from most because all I did was pour a fifth of Jack Daniels over a half gallon of Breyer's vanilla ice cream. It was not my recipe but one from someone we met once on a trip to New Orleans. His grandmother would make it for special occasions.

"What's that?" he asked.

"Milk punch," I said. "It's a southern tradition for New Year's Day. You have to try some."

"May we have some?" Aaron asked.

"It has booze in it," I looked at George.

"Let them try it. I don't think they will like it," he said.

I poured everyone a glass and handed it to them. As George predicted the boys hated it.

"Oh gross!" they said in unison.

"This is good," George said and downed his. "It reminds me of egg nog."

"That is what it's supposed to be," I said. "I think it was invented to take the hangover away from New Year's Eve."

"I'll have another," he said.

"Be careful. It packs quite a wallop," I said as I downed my third glass of the day.

"Just remember that starting tomorrow we go back on our diets," George said sipping his second glass of milk punch.

After dinner, I was in the kitchen cleaning up, while George and the boys were in the den watching television. I needed to keep myself occupied because I had imbibed too many glasses of milk punch.

The boys had turned off *The Twilight Zone* and had replaced it with Sponge Bob Squarepants and the volume was way up. I stepped out of the kitchen, and what I saw made me laugh to myself. Everyone was passed out. George and the boys were asleep on the sofa, and my dogs were at their feet. It was such a peaceful feeling to have my men in the house. I felt complete.

The sound of the phone ringing woke everybody, even the dogs.

"If you are finished playing, can you send my husband and children home, please?" It was Bella. "The boys have school in the morning and as much as I love my mother, she is finally leaving for Naples tomorrow."

"Yes, Bella. I will send them home pronto. Happy New Year."

"Thank you, Chick. Same to you," she added.

JANUARY IS THE best time of year to be in South Florida. The days are bright and sunny with a mild breeze blowing. I am now a native. When I would visit in the wintertime, I would dive in the ocean without a care, relishing the warmth. Now that I have become accustomed to the weather, I cannot even think about swimming for any length of time until May rolls around.

The alarm going off at five in the morning on January second was by far the most horrible sound in the world. I hit the snooze button that gave me nine more minutes of sleep. It did not help. The alarm sounded again. This time I sat up and turned off the damned thing. My feet were on the floor, but my head was in a cloud, and my mouth felt like an army had trudged through it. The only redeeming quality was the smell of the coffee brewing in the kitchen. I placed my hands on my knees and with a loud grunt, I managed a standing position.

"Oh boy," I said aloud. "Remind me to never make milk punch again."

I put on a clean jockstrap and gym shorts, went into the bathroom and brushed my teeth two times trying to remove the nasty taste in my mouth. I was walking to the kitchen when my phone rang. I knew it was George.

"Chick, I was afraid that you would be up," he said his voice more husky than usual.

"How you feeling?" I asked knowing the answer.

"Like shit and you?"

"The same."

"You wanna start our resolution tomorrow instead?"

"George, I love you," I said.

"I know."

He hung up and I went back to bed.

The next day was much better. The alarm clock sounded. I sat up turned it off, let the dogs out, used the bathroom, then walked into the kitchen where I poured a cup of coffee, added milk, then went back to the bedroom. In other words, it was just like any typical day, only I was happy.

George, as usual, met me out in front of the house. We jogged to Dale's gym where on this day we worked out chest and triceps. It felt good to break a sweat, as if all the toxins I put in my body during the holidays were leaving my body.

It was hard keeping my focus when I was lying on the bench looking up at George's crotch inches away from my face. The bar was loaded with two forty-five pound plates on either side. The bar weighed forty pounds. I was about to lift two hundred and twenty pounds.

"I want you to give me at least six reps," George commanded.

"You'll be with me, right?" I asked.

"Sure thing," he answered back. I looked up and he was smiling.

I wrapped my hands around the bar about shoulder width apart, took a deep breath, and lifted the bar. I slowly lowered the bar to my chest. It was really heavy. Once it touched my chest, I started to push the bar back up. That was one repetition.

"Good," George said. "Again."

Down went the bar with two hundred and twenty pounds to my chest. Slowly, I managed to lift it back up. I started to sweat.

"Again."

I lowered the bar to my chest, but this time it stayed there. I could not move it.

"Need some help?" he asked, looking down at me. All I could do was nod yes. He grabbed the bar between my hands and slowly pulled up. I know my face was red because it felt like it was on fire. With George's hands on the bar, we finished off three more reps, then locked the bar in place. I laid there on the bench like a wet dishcloth.

"How do you feel?" George asked.

"Great," I answered back. "Now it's your turn."

I kicked up from the bench and wiped it down with one of Dale's clean, white towels. George took my place on the bench.

"You want me to add any more weight, big guy?" I asked leaning on the bar.

"That would be a negative," he said. "What do you think I am, crazy?"

"Yes," I laughed.

George sat up, grabbed his towel, and using it like a whip he snapped it, the tip stinging my thigh.

"Ouch, you bitch," I exclaimed rubbing my leg where the towel whipped me. "Now lay down and give me at least six."

"Yes sir, Coach," George said. He laid on the bench, grabbed the bar, and with a deep breath lifted it. He brought the heavy weight down almost to his chest.

"That's one," I laughed.

"Oh hell," George exclaimed bringing the bar up just short of locking his elbows. He blew his breath out. He took a deep breath and brought the bar back down.

"Two," I counted.

"I know, I know!" his face was blood red.

George lowered and raised the bar three more times. Each time his face became redder and redder. I helped him a little on the last rep but he did most of the work. We locked the bar in place.

"You, George, are a beast!" I said in awe.

He could not say anything. He just laid there breathing hard. Finally, after several minutes, when he regained his composure, he declared, "Who's the bitch now?"

February

"I AM SO sore," George said rubbing his pectoral muscles. I started to laugh.

"What's so funny?" he asked.

"It reminded me of an old joke. You see Thor, the god of thunder, had come to visit New York City and met this little queen in the East Village. The queen says to the god of thunder, 'what's your name?' and he responds, 'I'm Thor!' The queen puts his hand on his hip and answers back, 'You think you're Thor, I'm tho Thor I can hardly thit!'"

I burst out laughing. George started to laugh though it made him hurt too much, and that made me laugh even more.

We had been working out harder than usual in the past few weeks. I had also begun to cook more at home. In fact, I was cooking for George and his family several nights a week. Bella was still not feeling well. I grilled chicken breasts and served them with brown rice and broccoli. I made a cheese sauce for the boys to pour over their greens. We ate fish, turkey, and occasionally, I fixed red meat. Like Ed, George had to have his red meat. It must have been a Cuban thing.

We ate tons of vegetables, either grilled, steamed, or roasted in the oven with olive oil and spices. We drank alcohol on special occasions. I began taking a small cooler to work filled with leftovers to eat throughout the day. I drank a gallon of water a day. The change in my physique was noticeable to everyone.

"George, where are your parents?" I asked one afternoon while we were running on the beach.

"Why do you ask?" he questioned.

"Well," I started. "You know all about me and my family. I see Bella's mother all the time. You never seem to talk about them."

"Not much to talk about, really. My mom and dad split up when I was very little. I lived with my mother until I was fifteen. She said I was uncontrollable and sent me to live with my father in St. Pete. That didn't last very long."

I didn't press him, just let him vent his feelings.

"Why was that?" I asked.

"We butted heads all the time. I was angry and he was lazy. When I was sixteen, I moved out. I have been on my own ever since. I showed them I could take care of myself. I didn't need them."

"Where are they now?"

"I don't know, and I don't care," he said with finality.

"Have they ever tried to get in touch with you?" I asked.

"Yeah, once my mother found our phone number and called right after Bella gave birth to Juan. Bella didn't know who she was. I told her my parents were dead."

"Dead? George why did you do that?"

"I didn't want anything to do with them. Why would they come looking for me? They didn't care about me when I was young."

"You don't think so?" I hoped I wasn't being too nosy.

"I know so. When I walked out of my father's house, he said in no uncertain terms that he was glad that I was out of his life."

"George," I said."I'm sorry."

"There's no need to be sorry," he said looking at me. "I can pick my family now, and I have you."

"And Bella."

"And Bella," he smiled.

"And the boys," I added.

"Yes, and the boys," he sighed.

"Come on, cry baby, I'll race you home," I said as I started to run as fast as I could.

"You're on, old man," he said. We were laughing and running wildly. If someone had seen us, he would have thought that we were crazy.

It was a long time since I'd gone shopping for St. Valentine's Day presents. Juan and Aaron were easy to buy for; all I needed was chocolate and lots of it. When it came to George and Bella, I wanted to be somewhat naughty. I went to the sex shop next to the strip joint in Hollywood. I am no prude but walking into the sex shop, I was slightly embarrassed. Okay, a whole lot embarrassed.

It was a large warehouse filled with all types of clothes, toys, DVDs, lotions, and potions. It took me a while to explore the aisles of fetish wear, but soon I became comfortable enough to have a good time.

I stopped at the selection of leather clothing and accessories. I picked up a studded black leather jock strap thinking how great George would look wearing it. What would Bella think of that? I placed it back on the rack. Then I saw exactly what I was looking for, a red satin thong. It was silly. George would turn as red as the thong, and Bella would laugh until she snorted. I also knew that later in the night after the boys were in bed, George would slip it on, and he would think how hot he looked in it. Bella would agree, as I know I would.

Bella, on the other hand, required something slightly more sophisticated, edible body powder perhaps. I knew that crotchless panties were out as well as mink lined handcuffs.

I strolled through the women's clothing when something caught my eye; a black fishnet, sleeveless hoodie. I examined it. No way would she wear something so revealing. I looked around to make sure no one was watching me, and I slowly walked over to the adult toy area. My face became hot, and I knew that I was blushing just being around all that latex. There were vibrators in many different colors and dildos of all shapes and sizes. I picked up one called The Big Dong. It was the size of my arm.

I scanned the section of nipple clamps, cock rings, butt plugs and ball stretchers. Nipple clamps maybe but ball stretchers? I thought to myself, who in their right mind would need those? Just wait a few years, guys, when you are fifty or so, and they would do that on their own. Thank God for tighty whities.

I had begun to perspire. Maybe I was a prude, for I gave up the idea that Bella needed something naughty as I left the store. Before exiting, however, I returned to the leather area and purchased the jockstrap for myself.

Once George and I were taken care of, I was off to Williams Sonoma to buy something for Bella that I knew she would like. The store was showcasing heart shaped kitchen utensils for the holiday. I chose a red heart cutting board and pancake turner. I would let George buy something sexy for her. For me being practical was the better option. Sue me, I'm a Virgo.

When I went over to George's, I saw that Bella had set up the dining room with red and pink balloons as well as red hearts. In the middle of the table were two heart shaped cakes, one pink the other blue.

"Bella, are you trying to tell me something?" I asked. I kissed her on the cheek, and placed my gifts on the table.

"Chick, I don't know what you are talking about," she said, smiling.

"Champagne?" She held up the bottle.

"Sure. Where's George?" I asked.

"Changing. Guess what he's wearing?"

"Don't tell me that Hawaiian shirt," I said with a grimace.

"Yup," she said. "He's had it on since this morning. I wish that it wasn't a holiday, so I didn't have to look at that horrible thing all day."

George as if on cue, walked into the dining room.

"What?" he asked looking from Bella to me then back to Bella.

I began to laugh.

"What's so funny?" George asked.

"Oh, nothing, honey," Bella giggled. "We were just discussing your wardrobe."

"What's wrong with it?" George asked twirling around so we could see it from every angle.

"Don't get me started."

George had grilled chicken drumsticks and thighs. He prepared a luscious green salad with hearts of palm and white rice. Once, we had eaten our dinner and the gifts were opened, George didn't wait to try on my gift. He came back into the dining room clad only in the red thong and sandals. He was stunning. His broad shoulders tapered down to a slim waist. The cheeks of his ass were hard and firm. The front of his thong was filled to the max.

I took a large gulp from my champagne.

The boys, Juan and Aaron, thought it was the funniest thing they had ever seen and laughed until they almost wet themselves.

"Oh my!" was all I could say.

"Cake anyone?" Bella said just in time.

March

ON THE WAY back home I said, "Friday there's an opener with the Yankees. I have tickets. Do you and the boys want to go?"

"Let me run it by the boss, but I'm sure it will be okay," he said.

Everything was fine with Bella. With George and the boys gone, she could take a Zumba class in the afternoon, if she felt up to it.

The Yankees in town meant that there was going to be a lot of action at the stadium, and all of us were very excited. I bought the boys Marlins t-shirts in the new black and teal colors.

It was a perfect evening for a ball game. The weather was cool and dry with long, thin clouds colored pink and gold as the sun was setting. The stadium was packed. We had seats right up front between third base and home plate.

"Dude, how did you get these seats?" George asked.

"Eddie gave them to me years ago," I said, "and I've always kept them. When did you start calling me Dude?"

"I don't know. It just seemed like the thing to do," he shrugged. I could tell that he was blushing. We both laughed.

"George, my man, tonight we do not worry about our diets. We will eat hot dogs with everything and drink beer, real beer, and I don't mean that watery light shit either," I said smiling.

We gave one another the high five. I ran up the steps to the concession area packed with people. It seemed to take forever, but I finally got everything I set out for—two beers, four smothered hot dogs, two sodas, two bottles of water—thank God for cargo shorts—and one box of Cracker Jacks®.

ON MY THIRTEENTH birthday, my father took me to see the Washington Senators. I knew that they were not the original team but what was referred to as an expansion team. They went from the National League to the American League. Many things had changed over the years like D.C. Stadium is now called R.F.K. Stadium, after Bobby Kennedy. There was some talk about getting rid of the team entirely, and I can remember my father saying, "All this money and D.C. can't keep a decent team."

It was the end of August, and the weather was hot and humid. The air was still and clothes hung on your body like damp laundry, but we were there to have fun. Pop had purchased seats in the shaded area. They were on the third base to home plate side, and they were so close, you felt like you could reach out and touch the players. Tonight was called Batting Cap Night and all kids under the age of twelve would receive a free batting cap. Pop had convinced one of the ticket takers to give me one because it was my birthday. It was made of cheap plastic. On the side was a drawing of a pitcher winding up in front of the Capitol. Because my father had given it to me, I loved it.

The game started and the players came out to shake hands. Pop said the uniforms had changed and they were now made of a material called polyester. It hugged the players' bodies tighter than the old style. At thirteen I could not keep my eyes off the bulges in their pants.

"Now listen," Pop would say, pointing to the catcher. "That was one of the positions I used to play. Not only is he the catcher, but he manages the whole game for his team. Now watch, he'll give the pitcher a signal of what pitch he thinks is best. Look, the pitcher says no. Now, yes!"

I had heard this from him a million times, but I didn't care because I loved hearing him talk about the sport. It is directly because of Pop that I am a big baseball fan to this day.

The pitcher nodded his head and threw a perfect curve ball.

"Strike one!" the umpire called out, elongating the words.

"Hot damn!" Pop yelled out, "that boy really knows how to toss that apple."

I loved the way he said things like stick for a bat or apple for a baseball. He had a way with words. I remember him referring to a Virginia State Trooper as a *state boy* more than once in my life.

The pitcher wound up and threw the ball, but this time wood met leather and with a line drive through centerfield, the batter landed on first base. The crowd stood and cheered.

"Now watch this," Pop gestured. "The pitcher is going to keep his eye on the first base and one eye on the batter."

The pitcher started his wind up. The player on first base took a couple of steps toward second. The pitcher put his foot down and turned his body toward first base. The runner went back, placed his foot on the base and put his hands on his hips as if to say "come and get me". The crowd cheered. The pitcher turned back to the batter then turned his head back to the runner who shrugged his shoulders as the crowd burst into laughter. The play resumed with the pitcher winding up; the runner took off for second base. This time the crowd was on its feet.

"Slide, slide," the crowd yelled.

The runner threw himself down and slid into second base in a cloud of dust.

"You are out!" the referee called, drawing out each word.

"What?" my father jumped out of his seat. "You've got to be kidding! That boy was safe by a mile!"

The Senators, of course lost, but I didn't care. Because my father had played for the original team after World War II, he did. I think that it was just a matter of pride.

Referring to my new batting cap, he said, "At least you have a little piece of history there, boy."

I loved it when he called me boy because I was the only one of his sons that he said that to. It was something between just him and me. When I became an adult, I still liked for him to say those words "I love you, boy," and I would say, "I love you too, Pop."

After Ed died, my father, at eight-five, insisted on flying to

Florida to attend the memorial service. My mother, my sister, and Pop flew into Fort Lauderdale Airport where our friend Sandi graciously picked them up and brought them to the house.

On the front porch, Pop, with the aid of his cane, hobbled up the steps and wrapped his arms around me and said, "I'll miss him too, boy."

"What am I going to do without him?" I asked my father.

"I promise you, things will get better."

GEORGE SAW ME coming down the steps with my arms filled with goodies.

"Boys, go help Uncle Chick; he has his hands full."

They came running up the steps to meet me. I handed them the hot dogs and the sodas. When the three of us returned to the seats, I handed George a beer.

"Is it a light?" he asked.

"Hell no!" I said. "We'll just have to either work out harder or run a little farther tomorrow. Okay?"

George said, with his hand on his hip, "If I get fat, I'll have you to thank."

"Ladies!" a guy shouted from two rows up. "Down in front. Some of us are trying to watch the girls."

He was talking about the Marlin Mermaids, a dance team, hired to entertain between innings and to act as cheerleaders.

I doubled over with laughter almost spilling my beer, and George turned blood red. I was still laughing when we sat down. The boys crawled on our laps, eating their hot dogs. Juan perched himself on his father's knee, mesmerized by the girls while Aaron sat all the way back on my lap with his back pressed up against my chest. I liked both of George's kids, but I especially liked Aaron, maybe because he was quiet and sensitive. Without being asked, he would take my hand whenever we were out or, like now, he would cuddle up close to me like he didn't want me to be alone.

I do not know if he liked being at the game or whether he just liked being out with us because he seemed more interested in his hot dog than he was with what was going on out on the field. I looked over at George and Juan, and thought how much alike they really were. Their profiles were so similar as they watched the Mermaids, both eating their hot dogs. Both of them were enthralled with the girls and the food, their jaws moving together in perfect unison. George looked over at me and was about to say something when he stopped and just smiled.

"What?" I asked.

"You'd have been a great father."

"I know."

"Those girls are pretty hot." George changed the subject.

"Yeah," Juan chimed back never taking his eyes off the girls.

George and I laughed. Aaron laughed too. I wrapped my arms around him and gave him a big squeeze.

"They are nice girls, too," I added.

"You know them?" he asked.

"They come into The Spa every now and then. I have actually given some of them massages."

"You lucky devil," George smirked. "I would love to have your job for just one day."

"I do some of the ball players too. I've always had a thing for jocks... or for things in jocks," I said laughing. George slapped me on the back of the head, and it made me laugh even harder.

Aaron was asleep by the end of the game, and George had thrown him over his shoulder. I had Juan by the hand as we all walked to the car. The sun had set hours ago, and the night was cool and crisp. We took our time walking to the car because we knew that it was going to be a mob scene trying to get out of the parking lot.

"I liked what you did at the seventh inning stretch," George said. "Pulling the Cracker Jacks® out during "Take me out to the Ball Game" was perfect. We all think you are a magician."

"No, you guys are the magic makers. I haven't had this much fun since my father took me to a ball game a long time ago," I said smiling down at Juan.

He smiled back. "Yeah, I had fun too."

Tears started to fill my eyes when George looked over at me. I turned my head away. He moved Aaron to his other shoulder and put his arm over my shoulder. I started to cry softly.

"Thank you," he whispered.

"No, George, thank you." I took a deep breath. "I am just an old fool," I said.

"Oh Chick, you aren't old."

I looked at him with mock indignation, and this time I slapped him on the back of the head. We laughed.

"Bella is pregnant," George blurted.

"What? I knew it!" I paused. "Are you happy?"

"You bet, I've always wanted a big family." I could tell, by his face, that he really was happy.

"You want another boy?" I asked.

"I know that Bella would like to have a little girl and between you and me, I would like to have a little girl too," he answered smiling.

"Is she going to quit working?" I asked.

"My wife is the most incredible person I know. She taught an aerobics class in the morning and gave birth to Aaron in the afternoon."

"How far along is she?"

"She just started her second trimester. We didn't want anyone to know until we were completely sure"

"I understand," I said. "That makes sense because she was sick throughout the holiday season."

"We knew then but chose not to say a thing, not even to Bernice and the boys. She said something to me about you mentioning that she looked pregnant."

"I didn't say she looked pregnant. I said that because she was nauseous all the time, I'd swear she was pregnant. It was supposed to be a joke."

"She thinks you are psychic," George said with a laugh.

WE WERE AT my house. It was Sunday afternoon, and the game was about to begin. I had made up a large batch of Buffalo wings with tons of celery, carrot sticks, and ranch dressing. The dogs were hanging out near the food, as always. I opened a couple of beers and took the snacks into the den, which looked out onto the backyard. I had no pool, but my patio was covered with beautiful potted plants that had once been neglected, but now were thriving because of my newfound tender, loving care.

"Oh boy!" Juan and Aaron said as they came running over to the tray of food. "Wings! Yay!"

I sat on the sofa. The boys filled their plates and crawled onto my lap. The dogs came over and laid down at our feet. The announcer on the TV was calling out the starting lineup. I looked over at George who was standing in the doorway of the kitchen, his muscular arms folded, just looking at the bunch of us. I realized suddenly that this is what I had been wanting my entire life.

THE BEST WAY to describe our house in Washington was a row house. It was not in the best area of town, but it was affordable. Built in 1893, it had three stories and was made of brick with black wrought iron bars on the windows and doors. An iron staircase led you to the front door. The living room and dining room had a large fireplace, and the ceiling was fourteen foot high. An exposed brick wall lent drama to the staircase going up to the second floor where there were two bedrooms, a bathroom, and a den with a skylight. The first floor, lower than street level, was an English basement or an efficiency apartment. As soon as we walked into the house, we knew we were home.

"Now that you boys own a house," Joyce exclaimed, "we need to make you legal. I'll see that it gets done right."

Joyce was one of my best clients and she lived in Old Town, Alexandria. Joyce was not what one would call small or shy, and she reminded me of Kathleen Turner. She had big hair, a big whiskey tenor voice, and, as a prominent attorney with aspirations of judgeship, she had a big presence.

Joyce made all the arrangements to have legal documents drawn up for Eddie and me. Since we were classified as single, we needed to have power of attorney and living wills so no one could take advantage of the survivor if something should happen to the other. That meant that our families could not come in and kick the living partner out of the house while he was still grieving, or ever, for that matter. She would have everything finalized in a few weeks. She decided that she would have a few people over to help celebrate with dinner, and we would sign the papers.

Joyce shared her house with Roy, who also practiced law. Roy was still married but was separated from his wife. It was very complicated. Joyce was so sharp in many ways but not, it seemed, in her love life. Who were we to judge her and her lifestyle? She was determined to attach Ed and me legally, and we were determined to let her do it even as we enjoyed her fabulous cooking.

Old Town is a colonial village that is just south of Washington. Most homes date back to the eighteenth century and are quite small, but very expensive. Joyce's was no exception. It was a two-bedroom townhouse, exquisitely decorated. She had set up a white iron table and chairs on the brick patio. The table was set with the finest of everything, with a huge bouquet of white Casablanca lilies in the middle of the table. Either she had good taste or Ed must have told her that they were my favorite flower.

Sitting on the patio with its vine-covered walls gave you the feeling that you were in New Orleans or Savannah. The moon was out and the weather was cool.

We dined on Cornish game hens with wild rice and baby vegetables. The wine, a white Bordeaux, from Roy's personal wine cellar, was nothing if not spectacular. Joyce finished off the evening with a beautiful flourless chocolate cake and champagne along with the necessary paperwork. Joyce and Roy explained each of the legal documents that we were signing and how we would use them.

"To my wonderful friends," I said after the papers were signed, notarized, and witnessed and the champagne was uncorked with a loud pop and much cheering. "This is as close to a wedding as I will ever have, and I want to thank everyone here. I propose a toast to Joyce and Roy for opening up their beautiful home and for taking a lot of their precious time to help us."

"Don't take any more of their precious time talking," Ed ordered and we all laughed. "Let's drink!"

"And," I said, trying to finish my speech, "for serving this expensive champagne. Last, but certainly not least to my loving and beautiful husband, whom I will always love forever. What a great way to begin our life journey together."

We all clinked glasses to the sounds of "here, here".

It did not take long before the papers came in handy. Ed was taken by ambulance to George Washington University Hospital because of a lung infection. I was at work, and he called me as soon as he was placed in his room. When I left him that morning, he had complained of a cold that he had had for some time but, as a nurse himself, he did not think it to be too serious.

It was a form of Legionnaires Disease but as a male who was single, the rapid diagnosis was, of course, PCP or a type of pneumonia that usually affects people with HIV. It took three days for his results to come back from the lab. He was HIV negative.

I left work and went straight to the hospital. When I reached his room, I was stopped at his door by a very large nurse. She was dressed in a traditional white dress, hat, and white wedge shoes that looked like they were two sizes too small for her feet. These shoes squeaked when she walked.

"Are you a relative?" she asked putting her fat hands on her wide hips and looking me in the eye.

"Ah, yes," I answered. "I am his partner."

"No, I mean, are you a blood relative?" she asked turning her back to me to check Ed's chart.

"Listen," I was beginning to become angry. "I told you that I was his partner. You know, like his husband."

She turned around slowly and with mock indignation said, "There is no need to be blasphemous. You can just take your gay right's parade right out of this hospital."

My blood was boiling. I looked at her name tag, A. McQueen. "Listen Nurse McQueen, I have legal papers at home declaring that I, and I alone, am responsible for the man in that room. Now if you want, I will go home and get those papers. When I return, I will be bringing my attorney with me and you will not like her."

Nurse McQueen pointed her finger at me with the nail coming dangerously close to slicing my nose when another nurse came walking down the hall. He had heard the commotion from the nurse's station. He took her arm and gently moved her out of the doorway. "Please let this man see his friend," he urged.

"Thank you" I mouthed as I stepped past the two of them. He led his co-worker by the shoulder back to the nurse's station. Her squeaky shoes masked the heated debate that ensued the entire way down the hall.

Ed was in his bed when I walked into the room. Even though he looked like death warmed over, he still had a smile for me. I took his hand and kissed it.

"It didn't take you long to force me to use those documents,"I said.

"JUST GET IN the car," George demanded. He had pulled into my driveway in his white sedan and opened the car window. "I've got an early meeting, so I'm going to have to shower at Dale's."

It felt strange to be driving to the gym because our usual routine was to jog, work out, then jog home. Once we entered the gym, we went right to work. With the lights, A/C, and the radio turned on, we began to warm up by hopping on two treadmills. Five minutes later, we were on the floor stretching.

"Well, Georgie, what are we going to work on today?" I asked.

"Today is Wednesday, so that means legs," George responded.

George always planned our workouts for us. He had a strict schedule for the week. Monday we worked on chest and Tuesday, back. Wednesday was dedicated to legs. Thursday was shoulders day and Friday, arms. We took the weekend off with the exception of the occasional short run. I have to admit that with all of George's hard work I was in the best shape of my life so if my best bud wanted me to do legs, then legs it would be.

To save space in a small gym like Dale's, you may find a multi-purpose unit called a Smith Machine which is equipped with a locking bar attached to a pulley system. Weights are placed on either side of the bar. With your shoulders placed under the bar, you push up and back to unlock it. As you do, your feet are slightly in front of your knees as you squat into a sitting position. The further into a sitting position, the better the work out. It is better to start off with light weights to warm up the muscles and joints. Some people wrap their knees with ace bandages for better support. I found that using heavy-duty knee sleeves did a much better job at protecting my soon to be fifty-year old knees. My legs, I felt, were the weakest part of my body. I told George that I wanted legs like his, and he told me that to get Latino legs I would have to pay for them.

George started things off by wrapping a towel around the bar for padding. He stepped up to the padding, placed his shoulders under it, stood up and unlocked the bar. He planted his feet about shoulder width apart and with his ass pushed out, he went into a sitting position. He went lower than ninety degrees, what you would call *in the hole*.

He counted out loud. Digging his heels into the ground, he shot back up into a standing position. He did it twelve times and each time he squatted, I watched his perfect form. He was wearing his usual black spandex shorts and white tank top but for this exercise, he buckled a wide black leather belt around his waist. I watched the muscles in his thighs and glutes strain against the weight. He shot the bar up and locked it into place. Now it was my turn. I walked up to the bar and looked at the weight on either side. I had done this amount of weight before, and I was comfortable with it.

"Here, put this on," George said. Taking off his wide belt and coming over to me, he placed it around my waist and latched it tightly. "This will give you some extra support." He slapped my backside. "Get going!"

My knee sleeves were down around my ankles, looking like some cheap leg warmers from the eighties. I pulled them up. With my shoulders firmly in place, I pushed up and unlocked the bar. With a wide stance, I planted my feet firmly in front of me. I took a deep breath, looked up, and slowly went into a sitting position feeling every muscle from my knees up strain under the weight. I counted two seconds in my mind, then shot back up for a count of one.

"Now, that's what I'm talking about!" George crowed. "You could not have been more picture perfect than that. You go, boy!"

I looked at him and mimicked, "You go boy?"

We both laughed.

"Get to it!" George commanded, snapping his fingers. "I've got to get to work, remember?"

We got to it all right. I finished my set of twelve, then George doubled the weight. I handed him the belt, and he strapped it on, tighter this time. He stepped up to the bar, lifted it on his shoulders, unlocked it, and squatted down. This time holding the weight for a count of two was a little harder, but we both prevailed. First him, then me. George again doubled the weight, and the belt was buckled even tighter. This time George could only press out six squats. He was covered in sweat so that you could see through his shirt to the beautiful skin beneath.

"Your turn," he panted, taking a drink of water.

"All right," I shrugged. "I don't know if I've done this much weight before."

"That's okay. I'm here to help you."

I went over to the bar and I could smell George's sweat on the towel that he had wrapped around the bar. That was a good thing. I inhaled his masculine aroma deeply, hoping it would give me the added strength that I needed to handle this much poundage. I placed the bar on my shoulders as I stood and unlocked the bar. I felt the weight heavy on my shoulders.

"You okay?" George asked.

"Yep." It was all I could say.

"Go for six,"

I planted my feet with a wide stance. I took a deep breath. I looked up. I slowly went into a sitting position. I counted, one, pause, two then with all my might, I pushed myself back up.

"Good, again," he directed.

I did it again.

"Again."

I did it again. I felt my quads and glutes starting to burn.

"You okay?"

I nodded.

"Again." He was intense.

Sweat was pouring off me. I was breathing hard, and my face was turning red, but I was not about to quit. I saw George do six perfect squats even though he was ten years younger than I.

"I'm with you all the way," he whispered in my ear. With his help, I finished my last two repetitions.

He explained to me how to assist in heavy squatting. "The one in the back helps out getting past the sticking point. Just wrap your arms around your buddy's rib cage and take an extra wide stance. When they can't make it, just push with your legs to get them back up. You want to try it?"

"Sure," I answered.

George added twenty-five pounds to each side of the bar. He looked at me and winked as he tightened the belt around his waist. He went around to the bar and put his shoulder to it, then lifted and unlocked it. I positioned my feet a little further than shoulder width apart, just like George had done moments before and wrapped my arms around his chest. We both were soaking wet with sweat. In front of us was a floor to ceiling mirror, and all you could see was George with an extra pair of arms around him and four legs instead of two. He slowly went into a sitting position while I was holding on to him. When he reached the point where his thighs were parallel to the ground, he pushed back onto my crotch and counted out loud. "One, two. Up!" he cried and up we went.

"You okay?" he asked.

"Oh, yeah!"

"Again!" Down we went and when we reached the bottom, George did the same thing, he sat back right on my crotch. "One, two," he counted out loud. With a loud grunt, we both shot back up again.

Both of us were out of breath yet George asked, "Again?"

"If you can, I can," I gasped.

Down we went again. We stopped at the bottom, and he counted to two again. I liked the feel of his hard ass on the front of my shorts.

"Don't you want to count to four this time?" I whispered in his ear. He laughed so hard we almost didn't get the bar back up and locked. We both fell onto the floor, panting and sweating.

"Now it's your turn," George said breathless. "And this will be the last one because I've got to go."

"I've never done this much weight before," I panted.

"Don't worry I'm right behind you," he reminded me as he slapped my ass.

I calculated the weight on the bar, and it was just shy of four hundred pounds. George removed the belt from his waist and placed it around my body, just beneath my rib cage. He looked me in the eye as he buckled it very tightly. For the last time today, I stepped up to the bar and with a loud grunt, lifted it onto my shoulders and unlocked it.

"Are you ready?"

"Yep," I answered.

George wrapped his arms around me from behind. He planted his feet widely but firmly on the floor like a Sumo wrestler.

"Let's do it," he ordered.

I could feel my heart beat in my chest and my throat go dry. I went into a sitting position, and I felt George's crotch pushing on the back of my shorts. He whispered in my ear the count of two. I kept my eyes up and pushing with my heels, I drove the heavy bar back up. Sweat was pouring off my face and I was breathing hard.

"You okay?" he asked.

"Yep."

"Again?"

"You bet."

With George's arms around me in a vice grip and his muscular legs to help support the both of us, I knew that we could do this. I went into a sitting position, again I felt his hot groin pressing into the seat of my shorts. This time I felt he was beginning to get hard.

Oh boy, I thought.

"Up," he growled. I pushed with my heels and up we went. Both of us covered with sweat and breathing hard. "Again!"

"You bet," I murmured between gulps of air.

We went down together; this time there was no mistaking his erection.

"Up," he commanded and up we went.

With the bar still on my shoulders and my arms stretched out, I looked in the mirror. George's arms were still around my body when he peeked out over my shoulder.

"Is there something you want to tell me?" I asked between breaths.

"Well," he said, gasping for air. "Let's just say I don't have a gun in my pocket."

We looked in the mirror at one another for a long second. Together we burst out laughing.

The lights went on in the front room.

"What's going on in there?"

"It's Dale," George said. "Hey, it's me, George."

"And Chick," I added.

"And Chick," George added loudly. "Come on," he motioned to me, "let's go say hi."

"I can't meet him looking like this," I refused. "I'm a mess."

"Believe me, he won't mind a bit," George said. We walked into the front room.

Dale was standing at the front desk. He was my height and extremely well built with reddish hair that was graying at the temples. His massive arms were covered with freckles. He was wearing a red tank top with "Dale's Gym" and a caricature of himself, complete with his flat top haircut, printed on the front. His gray, cotton shorts were stretched tightly across his body because of his huge thigh muscles. I could not keep my eyes from wandering down his legs to his calves, which looked like bowling pins. Slowly I looked back up. His face broke into a broad, white smile. I finally found his eyes. They were green, just like mine.

I felt as if I had been caught doing something naughty, and my face began to feel warm; I knew that I was blushing.

Dale was leaning on the desk with his hand on his hip and one leg crossed in front of the other. He seemed to give us both the once over before he opened his mouth.

"What are you boys up to?" he asked still smiling. "You two almost look like you've been fucking."

George and I looked at one another and just started laughing.

"What? Did I say something funny?" Dale asked.

"No, we were just finishing legs when you turned on the lights," George said.

"I bet you were," Dale said, keeping his eyes on me.

"Dale, this is Chester," George said.

"Nice to meet you," I said walking over to him and holding out my hand for him to shake. "Please call me Chick."

His handshake was strong and friendly.

"Oh, so this is the Chick that I've been hearing about. Bella has been telling me about her two husbands. You must be the one that cooks."

Still holding on to Dale's hand, I must have blushed again. I could see why everyone liked him; he was a great big teddy bear. "That would be me, I guess."

"Listen," George said. "I've got to hit the shower and go to work. I'll see you guys later."

He disappeared around the corner, and I stayed to talk to Dale. I found out that he had grown up in Madison, Wisconsin. He sounded like he had a Midwest twang. As he talked, I looked at the photographs behind him, of body builders, and realized that they were all of him winning awards. In one shot, he had his arms up holding a giant, golden trophy.

"Are those pictures of you?" I asked.

"Yeah," he answered modestly. He pointed to the pictures on the wall. "That is when I took Mr. Wisconsin in ninety-five and here," he took a picture off the wall and handed it to me, "is where I took the title of Mr. America in ninety-six. It was something that I'd wanted ever since I was a kid."

I held the framed photo in my hand and just stared at it. "You are awesome," I drooled.

"Those days are long gone," he sighed.

"What do you mean?" I asked. "You still look great."

"I turned fifty-three this year, and everything has begun to rust on me, my back, my knees."

"I know what you mean. I'm turning fifty in August, and I am bound and determined to go into the second half of my life kicking and screaming."

"You look great."

"Thanks," I said. I noticed that Dale was wearing a gold ring on his right hand just like Eddie and I wore.

IT HAD BEEN Christmas time in Washington, D.C., and a blanket of snow had covered the ground. It was beautiful for only a few hours because in the city, snow becomes very gray in a short period of time.

A business card had been left on the windshield of my car, X-mas trees for sale. At the bottom was the address and hours between five and ten in the evening. Something sounded very strange; however, we hopped in our Isuzu Trooper and headed for the address on the card. It turned out to be a vacant lot in a seedy section of town. It was fenced in with a string of naked light bulbs hanging over the lot. We sat bundled in the car trying to gather up our courage. No one had entered or left the lot. Finally, after what seemed like hours, a car approached then stopped. A young couple got out of the car and disappeared into the trees. If it was good enough for them, then it was good enough for us. We stepped out of the car and walked across the windy street. When we approached, a nice looking man came over to greet us. He informed us that all the trees in the lot were twenty bucks and since the ceiling in our house was high, we took the tallest tree we could find. He even helped us tie the tree onto the top of the car. We handed him twenty-five dollars and away we went as fast as we could, maneuvering dangerously on cold and wet city streets. It was about five blocks later before we could breathe.

"I feel like I just bought a hot tree on the coldest night," I exhaled.

Ed responded, "That, or we pulled off some kind of drug deal." We both started laughing and heaved a sigh of relief.

The tree turned out to be the prettiest tree that we had ever purchased, and it fit perfectly in the bay front of the house.

Christmas day was cold but sunny. Tiny swirls of snow danced up deserted streets, and puffs of chimney smoke blew from rooftops all across the city. Everyone was either relaxing for the holiday or enjoying a much-needed day off. We had a fire burning in the fireplace, and the tree was lit. With lulling holiday music on the stereo, the bottle of Tattinger Rose champagne was nearly gone by the time we finished opening our gifts. I always liked to put something extra special in the toe of the stocking since it was be the last gift to be opened. This year I had bought Ed a gold band.

"What's this?" he asked holding up a small gift wrapped in gold foil.

"A little something," I hinted.

He opened the box, took out the ring, and held it out to examine it. I took the ring from him and went down on one knee.

"Ed, from the first moment I saw you, I knew that we would be together forever. Some day it might be legal for gay people to marry. I know that I don't need a ceremony to celebrate our love for one another; we show one another that every day. Will you wear this ring as a symbol of our love for one another?"

"Yes," was all he could say as tears filled his big, brown eyes.

We chose to wear our rings on our right hands to show that our love is visible but different.

"OH, MY GOD, just look at the time," I said as I looked at the clock behind Dale. "I've got to get to work."

"What do you do?" Dale asked.

"I'm the manager of The Spa on South Beach," I said. "I do some massage, but mostly I just tell people what to do."

"Could you give me a massage? I sure could use one."

"Sure," I grinned.

"Really? Most massage people are intimidated by my size."

Taking in the whole scope of him and thinking to myself what it would be like to have my hands all over that massive torso of his, I could only imagine what his hard muscles would feel like. I could feel an erection beginning to grow.

"I'm not afraid of big," I divulged.

"No, I bet you aren't," he answered, smiling.

As I walked over towards the locker room, I looked back. Dale was following me with his eyes, and we both smiled. When I returned home, I was going to need a cold shower.

George had just pulled the curtain open and was reaching for his towel when I walked into the locker room. Shining wet, his smooth, almost hairless, long muscular body looked perfect. From being outside, his honey-colored skin had darkened, and I thought if I licked his skin, it would taste like warm *café con leche*. The tan line from his shorts showed how much his color had changed. His cock and scrotum were several shades darker than the rest of his body and like most Latin men, he was uncircumcised. I could not keep my eyes off him, and he stood there letting me. He opened up his arms and turned around so that I could see all of him. He shrugged his shoulders as if to say, "Eh, not too bad."

I grabbed my keys, ran out the back door and did not stop until I reached my house.

In the shower, I could not stop visualizing both men and how different they were. There was Dale with his big hard muscles that looked like they were made of stone. Then there was George's sinuous body and the thought that earlier he had wrapped his sweaty arms around my body and pressed his hard cock against the back of my shorts. I took my erection in both hands and brought myself off. It was the most intense orgasm I had had in a very long time.

April

I CAME HOME from work one day to find George sitting on my front porch. I have two white wooden rockers that Eddie and I purchased years ago for our retirement. With a cocktail in his hand, Ed loved to sit in the rocker, especially in the evening, watching the world go by. Now George was sitting in Ed's chair.

How different two people can be and at the same time resemble one another. Ed was heavy with lots of hair everywhere, except his head. He was not athletic, but he was very strong.

George, on the other hand was trim, his body athletic and muscular, like a tiger. Watching him sit and rock back and forth still reminded me so much of Ed.

Something was on George's mind, and he needed to talk. Translated, that meant that George needed to run. Men are not exceptionally big talkers, but if you give them some kind of strenuous activity to do, it will open them up.

"Let me change my clothes, and I'll be right with you," I offered.

I unlocked the door and was greeted by the boys in their usual poodle frenzy. I realized that by just going to the back door and opening it up without saying a word, both of my dogs were calmer.

I let them out into the backyard, closed the door, and went into the bedroom to change. I threw the bag, with all my stuff in it onto the bed as George came into the room and sat down.

"What's up?" I asked.

"Bella is driving me nuts!" he blasted.

"What did you do?"

"What do you mean what did I do?" he sounded frustrated.

"George," I said, "Bella is pregnant. She is going to have her moments. Wasn't she like this with the boys?"

"No, not at all," he explained. "Next week is her birthday, and I don't know what to do for her. She seems to hate everything and everybody, including me. That's why I came up here to get away from things for awhile."

"She sounds like she could use a massage. Hey, what about me?" I asked.

"What do you mean, you?"

"Hello," I drawled out. "What do I do for a living?"

"Oh, yeah," he said thinking. "You can massage a pregnant woman?"

"Sure. I have a special table and everything. I'll give her a facial too, and I'll get one of the girls to do her nails. She'll love it!"

"She would like that," he seemed relieved.

I was undressing while we talked and was down to my underwear. I thought to myself that I had seen George naked so he might as well see me in the raw too. I dropped my skivvies and was reaching for a jockstrap when George said, "You look good."

"Thanks," I said, "but it's mostly because of you."

"I hope that I look half as good as you when I finally reach your age," he said laughing. I threw my underwear at him.

It was the beginning of April, but the evening was hot. Even the breeze from the ocean could not cool things down. I knew that George needed to vent, and I let him talk the entire run to the beach and back. It's funny what problems can be solved in thirty minutes.

"Dale is out of town for a few weeks," George said. "Bella is watching the gym and teaching classes. She is not happy."

"Why do you think that is?" I asked in my best therapist voice.

"Everything bothers her. Her back hurts, she's nauseous, and everything makes her sick, even me. She won't let me come near her. When she was pregnant with the boys, we had sex all the time. She said it was good for the babies to know that their parents still loved one another. Not this time," he protested.

Trying to change the conversation, I asked, "Where's Dale?"

"He went back to Wisconsin to wrap up a few things."

"Like what?" I asked.

"I'll let him tell you when he gets back. Bella wants to have you both over for dinner one night."

"Oh yeah? What's the occasion?"

"Nothing. She just wants you guys to really get to know one another."

"I swear, George," I said, "both of you are like two yentas."

"Yeah, I know."

BELLA WAS ALL excited about her *day of beauty* as she called it. We were going to start with the facial, then go into the massage. I could do both services in the same room. I introduced her to everyone. She loved the facility and wondered why it had taken her so long to get there.

"I guess that you were just waiting for me," I said, teasing her.

"You are probably right," she said. She had changed out of her street clothes and had settled down on the facial bed to be pampered. Bella took in a long deep breath and let it out. "You don't know how much I needed this. I have been a real bitch lately."

"It's going to be all right. You are with me now," I said.

George was right; her appearance had changed. Her skin had lost its color, and her hair had become dry and brittle. "I'm going to fix you right up."

I knew that I needed to stay away from strong aromas because of her pregnancy and knowing that she would be sensitive to smells, I chose light and gentle aromas like rose and lavender. I treated her feet with Dead Sea salt. I massaged in a cream that I had made with peppermint, and next I wrapped her feet in warm towels. I massaged her scalp with a combination of olive and jojoba oils. Finally, I took her hands and applied a cream with the sweet smell of tangerine. At that point, she was like putty in my hands. She took another deep sigh of relief and melted into the table.

"You know, I've never had a man give me a facial before. You have the nicest touch." She cleared her throat. "My boys just love you. They call you Uncle Chick. Isn't that sweet? You know how much George likes you. He thinks of you like the brother he never had. You see, George was an only child and his mom and dad divorced when he was very young. Neither one of them remarried. That's why I think George wants a big family so he will never be lonely again."

"He has a big, um, heart."

"Yeah," she giggled, "and other things, too. He has a lot of love for a lot of people. You know when I first met him I thought he was gay."

That statement took me by surprise. "You did?"

"I thought you might like that. He was so well mannered and good-looking. He dressed in tight clothes and always hung around with other guys, all the time."

"How did you guys meet?" I asked curiously.

"At the gym. He took one of my classes. When I saw him in those damn tight, spandex shorts, I couldn't keep my eyes off of him, so I asked *him* out." She put the emphasis on him. "We went out a couple of times, and he never even touched me. Not even a good night kiss. I remember one night he walked me up to my door, opened it, and said good night. Out of total frustration, I asked him, are you gay?"

"What did he say?"

"He didn't know what to say at first. He told me that he liked me very much but that he didn't want to force me into anything I might not want to do. He said that I was beautiful and sexy, and I had the best ass he had ever seen in a pair of shorts. Finally, he admitted to me that he had not been with a lot of women, and he was afraid of disappointing me."

"What did you do?" I whispered, lost in the moment she was describing.

"I started crying and he kissed me. He lifted up my chin and kissed me gently on the cheek as if he were tasting my tears. When my mouth met his, he put his arms around me, and I knew at that moment that we would be together for the rest of our lives. I dragged him into my house and did him, right there in the entry way."

"Way to go, Bella! I'm proud of you."

"Yup, I'm a slut, but George stayed the whole night. In fact, he never really left. We were married a month later. A small ceremony at city hall in front of a judge. I wish my father was still alive; he would love to have George as a son-in-law. My mother was the only witness. Of course I wore white."

Even with the bright green seaweed masque applied, very

thickly to her face, I could tell she was smiling.

I liked Bella more at that moment than I had even thought possible.

A few hours later, Bella was resting in the lounge wearing one of the spa's thick white robes, sipping a cup of herbal tea. Her feet were up on the ottoman in front of her, and her eyes were closed. A total transition from the stressed out Bella of earlier in the day.

"I love the color on your nails," I observed.

"Jungle red," she answered. "Oh, Chick, I don't want this day to end. Thank you so much for this glorious present."

"It was really my pleasure. Now will you do something for me?" I had a little trick up my sleeve.

"Sure, anything," she purred.

"I just want to check something out," I smiled.

"Okay," she said a little nervously

"It's nothing, Bella. Just sit up naturally."

She lifted up her head and moved her feet off the ottoman.

"Look straight ahead."

As she looked forward, I pulled her bottom left eyelid down. I saw two bright red veins but they did not come together to create a triangle or trident. Bella was going to have a girl.

"You are going to get your wish," I assured her.

"What do you mean?" she asked.

"Let's just say you better get George to paint the baby's room pink."

"Really?" she exclaimed. "How do you know?"

"It's something that a *Mohel* showed me. He is very spiritual. I love his wife too."

I realized at that point that the two of us were sitting there holding hands like old girlfriends.

"You know, Chester, Dale likes you," she changed the subject.

"Yeah, how do you know that?" I asked.

"He told me," she chuckled.

"But he wears a ring."

She sat up and looked me in the eye. "So do you."

I immediately looked at my right hand, "Yeah, I do."

"Sometimes you men can be so stupid," she declared.

I had to agree.

I remembered those last days with Ed in the hospital, his legs filled with edema. I massaged his limbs trying to rid them of fluid back up. The slightest touch could be painful, but he was happy that someone, especially me, was touching him. Sometimes at night, I still missed the feel of him.

IT WAS NOT Friday, but Monday the thirteenth, that started a very emotional week for me. I had the boys groomed, and they looked beautiful. Whenever they came home from the groomer, I could not keep my hands off them because their coats were so soft; just like crushed velvet. Francisco, the groomer, liked to spray them with French lavender. He said it calmed them down. I was loving them when I noticed some rather large lumps on Thom. I thought that maybe he had had some reaction to the spray that Francisco used. In the morning, the lumps were still there so I decided to call the vet and take Thom in.

In my heart, I already knew what was wrong. Later that day, a dreaded phone call confirmed my fear.

"The doctor wants to speak with you when you come in," the receptionist said.

I left work immediately and headed for the doctor's office. The entire drive was a nightmare. I hated Miami streets at rush hour. By the time I parked my car, I was covered in sweat. I was quickly escorted to a room where they brought Thom to me. He was so happy to see me. I sat down on the floor and let him lick my face.

"Are you okay, buddy?" I asked Thom.

The doctor, Michael, walked into the room and sat down on the chair next to where we were sitting on the floor. He was short and stocky wearing scrubs like a surgeon, his short sleeves rolled up to show off his biceps. I had always liked him. He was friendly and talkative. Mostly, I trusted him. He held Thom's file in his hands, and he sighed; a bad sign.

"Thom has lymphoma," he blurted. There it was said. "It is a very aggressive form of the disease. Have you noticed anything different about him? Any changes?"

"He doesn't want to get up in the morning, but I thought it was just because he was old. One of the dogs has been getting sick lately," I recalled.

"What color is it?" he queried.

"Yellowish."

"I thought so because he's thrown up a lot since he's been here," he added sadly.

I called him by his first name. "Michael, what should I do?"

"Chester, I've always been straight with you, knowing all that you've been through the past few years, but..."

He lowered his eyes.

"If it were my dog, considering his age, I wouldn't put him through chemotherapy. It can be very tough on an older dog. I don't think that he will make it through the week."

He dropped his head to his chest and whispered, "If he were my own pet, I would put him down."

The silence was so thick you could cut it with a knife. I could not believe what I was hearing. I hadn't realized that I had stopped breathing.

"He has been with me for over eleven years," I exploded, bursting into tears. "I named him after our good friend Thomas who died from HIV."

"I am terribly sorry," he consoled. "I truly am."

He placed his hand on my shoulder.

He explained the procedure to me, and I told him that I wanted to be with Thom when it happened. He agreed with me and left the room to give us time alone.

"I am so sorry, Thom," I sobbed. "You have been such a good friend. Why does God have to take everyone that I love away from me?"

Sitting on the floor, I started to rock him in my arms. I looked him in the eyes, and I could see the pain. I brushed the curly hair on his head with my hands. He closed his eyes and laid his head back onto my arm.

The doctor and his assistant entered the room. The assistant took Thom from me and placed him on the metal table. The doctor expelled a deep sigh; I could tell that this was the part of his job that he hated the most. He placed the needle into Thom's front leg and administered the drug that would stop his heart.

"It should only take a few minutes," the doctor whispered.

I laid my face close to my faithful friend's head and while I stroked his red curly coat, I kept repeating over and over *I'm so sorry,* until I felt him breathe his last breath. My beautiful Thom was gone. I sobbed. All the emotion that I had been holding inside of me for more than two years took over, and I wept uncontrollably. I cried for everything and for everyone that I had lost.

"It's over." The doctor said kindly. "He's no longer in pain."

He walked around the table, put his arms around me, and held me tightly. I had never been treated with such respect from a veterinarian or any doctor, for that matter, before, and I put my arms around his shoulders and cried.

"I am so sorry," he repeated.

After some time, the assistant handed me Thom's collar and leash. I was gently escorted out the backdoor with a handful of tissues. I went to my car, and sitting in the front seat, I simply did not know what to do. I needed to talk to someone. I called George's home number. The phone rang six times before someone answered it.

"Chick, what is it," Bella asked.

"I had to put Thom down," I cried, speaking incoherently.

"Chick, I can hardly understand you. Did you just say you put Thom down?"

"I did, just now," I was trying to catch my breath.

"Why, Chick, what happened?"

I told Bella what the doctor had told me, that Thom was very ill, that I shouldn't let him suffer. After talking with Bella, I felt better, at least well enough to drive home. Jerry was waiting for me at the front door, and as I saw him, my tears began anew.

"Well, it looks like it's just you and me, Jerry," I let him out the backdoor and stood there watching him. He was peacefully oblivious to everything that had occurred as he lifted his leg and peed. And for that I was grateful.

IT HAD BEEN October when our friend, Thomas came to visit us from DC. He was a handsome man and always impeccably groomed. When he walked into the house, I immediately noticed he was much thinner than I remembered. His skin, too, was ashen, his hair much thinner and the twinkle in his eye extinguished. He had become weak and frail; in other words, he was dying.

"I know that I don't have long," he confirmed my thoughts. "I just want to have fun, okay?"

"Sure, anything you want," Ed promised.

Ed and Thomas were very close, and they could talk about everything. Ed never revealed what they talked about to anyone, and that meant me too. That was the kind of friend Ed was to everybody, but especially to Thomas.

The entire week that Thomas was with us, he mostly slept and ate, but very little. He did look forward to cocktail hour, which at our house could start at any time. One evening towards the end of his stay, we were in the den looking out onto the backyard.

"I am so happy for the two of you," Thomas' voice was small and frail. "Your house is so welcoming. I want to thank you for being such good friends to me and showing me such a good time." You could tell there was something else on his mind as he searched for the right words."My mother wants me to move to a hospital near her, but I don't want to go."

"Tell her that you don't want to go," Ed reasoned.

"It's no use. When Mother makes up her mind about something there is no changing it."

I could relate to that.

It was sad to see the life of our friend taken away from him at such a young age. I do not think that he was forty when he passed away. We were pleased that he wanted to spend some quality time with us in Florida before his time would come. Eventually, though, we had to take him to the airport and send him home. We helped him with his luggage at the airport and from there, a friendly flight attendant helped him onto the plane. Ed and I did not say a word to one another the entire drive home from the airport.

At the beginning of February, Thomas called to tell us that he was permanently moving to a facility in North Carolina, near his mother and stepfather. He was still not happy about the situation, but his mother thought it was best for him to be close, and truthfully, he was tired of arguing. Mercifully, Thomas died in his own bed in DC the day before Valentine's Day. At least he did not die in that hospital bed; that was the thing he dreaded most.

I HAD BROUGHT Jerry up into the bed with me and was lying on my side with both arms around him. I heard the front door open and then close. George was still in his uniform, a gray polo shirt with Miami Dade Fire and Rescue in large letters on the back and plain navy cargo pants. He removed his boots and slid next to me on the bed. With both of us on our sides, he placed one arm around my shoulder and one around my chest. He pulled himself even closer to me, and whispered in my ear, "I am so sorry for you, Chick."

We stayed like that for a very long time.

May

HER NAME IS Leslie, but she goes by the stage name of Bambi; Bambi LaFleur. It was an ordinary afternoon, but one we would not soon forget. We were sitting at our favorite bar on Lincoln Road. It was our South Beach version of Cheers because everyone really did know your name.

It was Happy Hour and that meant either two for one or three for one or all for one and one for all, but we were the only two people in the bar when this vision walked through the front door. She is one part Marilyn Monroe, one part Jayne Mansfield, one part Mamie Van Doren, and the rest Milton Berle and Mom's apple pie all wrapped into one amazing package. For all of us it was love at first sight.

Bambi was there to make some deals with the local bar owners to let her perform in their clubs. She is an entertainer and her shtick is a humorous take on lounge singers of the fifties and sixties, and the kicker was, she writes and sings all her own music. She will also take requests. Her meeting over, she shimmied up to the bar and ordered what she called a Bambi Banger, a vodka and soda with a splash of grenadine.

"Any one of you boys got a smoke?" she asked, her hand on her hip and her foot on the bar rail.

"Sure, anything for a pretty girl like you," I oozed.

She smiled her famous crooked smile and sat down with us. Many cocktails later, we were the best of friends.

She was from Great Falls, Montana. The day after she graduated from high school, she packed one bag and moved to Milan, Italy, to work as a plus-sized model. She did very well for herself for the ten years that she was there, but when it was time to leave, she left to resume her dream of being an entertainer. She is an excellent singer and entertainer as well as one of the best Marilyn Monroe impersonators in the country.

I was working in a salon, and had not started at The Spa yet. One day, one of those days filled with drama, when I finally reached home, someone had parked his or her big Cadillac El Dorado in my space in the driveway. I was not happy, but it all changed when I walked in the door. Sitting in my living room was Marilyn Monroe, drinking a martini. How could you be angry at that?

When Ed turned forty, we threw a party for him. There was a Barbra Streisand female impersonator who sang Ed's favorite Barbra song, "I've Never Been a Woman Before," while sitting on his knee.

Bambi wanted to know if Eddie liked any of the songs that she sang. We were her most devoted fans and had pretty much seen her perform all over the city.

"Satin Doll," he told her.

Without missing a beat, as if on cue, she started to sing acapella:

> Cigarette holder which wigs me.
> Over her shoulder she digs me.
> Out cattin' that satin doll.
> Baby, shall we go out skippin'?
> Careful, amigo, you're flippin',
> Speaks Latin that satin doll

Years later she would sing that song again, but for a different reason.

Ed did not want to be buried, nor did he want a funeral. We both stated in our living wills that we wanted to be cremated with our ashes scattered over the waters of Key West. We had spent many fun-filled days and nights in the Conch Republic.

Once, we stayed at a guesthouse, The Orleans House, on Duval Street. The main house was two stories with a clothing optional sun deck on the roof. My experience was that the ones on the top deck should never have their clothes off.

The bigger rooms or suites were on the second floor, and the rooms to the back of the house had balconies that looked over the pool and spa deck. The rooms on the ground level looked right into the pool. A high wooden privacy fence covered in multiple colors of bougainvillea shaded the pool and deck. The setting was quiet and private, even though there was plenty of coming and going.

On this particular evening, we were entertained by the pool with a fashion show by a local men's wear designer. The champagne was cold, the evening humid, and the attire minimal. The models were wearing the skimpiest of swimwear and were socializing nicely with the guests. That is when Ed thought it best that we leave and find some other, less engaging, activity.

We went to a bar to have more drinks and we ran into one of the guests, Ray, from the pool deck. Ray told the two of us that he was raised in the Midwest and he was not accustomed to so many gay men and was a proverbial kid in a candy store. He was extremely animated from large amounts of alcohol. When he found out that Ed was from Cuba, he pushed himself between us, turned his back to me, and with his elbows on the bar, looked at Ed with big, puppy dog eyes.

"You are very handsome," Ray slurred.

"Thank you very much and you are very drunk," Ed answered, smiling.

"Yes, I am. Where are you staying?" he asked.

"The same place you are. Don't you remember us from the pool?" Ed questioned.

"Who's us?" Ray said turning around to face me. "Well, hello, who are you?"

"I'm Chick and I'm with him," I pointed to Ed.

He looked back over to Ed and then back to me. "You guys are awfully lucky to be together. Let me buy you a drink," he offered congenially. He turned quickly to catch the bartender's gaze and almost fell over.

"That's okay," I told him. "We were just leaving."

"What do you mean? You just got here," he gestured toward the bar.

"Yeah," Ed agreed. "We just got here."

We let Ray buy drinks for us. I noticed Ray's hand on Ed's thigh, and I wondered how long it would take Ed to realize it too. He seemed very comfortable with Ray's attention. He let Ray buy several rounds of drinks for us.

"Did you know that Chick here is from Virginia?"

"I love Southern boys," Ray snorted. He threw his arms around me as if he had not seen me in a very long time.

"Time to go," Ed announced. He grabbed my hand as he led me out of the bar.

"What was that all about?" I asked as Ed and I walked toward the guesthouse.

"He was drunk and obnoxious," Ed responded.

"It was okay when it was all about you but when his attention turned to me, it was time to go, right?"

"That's not it at all and you know it. It was just time to go. Now that we are back at the guesthouse, let's just go to our room and go to sleep." Ed stated as we walked onto the pool deck.

"You know what?" I giggled, looking around. "There is no one out here, so let's get naked and jump in the pool."

Without waiting for him to answer me, I pulled off my shirt, dropped my shorts, kicked off my flip-flops, and jumped into the pool. The next thing I knew the entire pool was filled with naked men splashing all around. Ed acted as if I had orchestrated the whole thing, stormed up the staircase to our room, and loudly locked the door.

One of the men was Ray, who was standing by the sign that said, NO DIVING. He, of course, dove headfirst into the pool. Ray came up from the water. His face had been scraped very badly by the pool bottom and he was bleeding profusely. I quickly helped him out of the pool and sat him down on one of the lounge chairs.

"You stay here, I'll get help," I told Ray, who was slumped over in the chair. I thought to myself, as I looked at the damage to his face, it was not too bad and that he would live, but he really was going to hate himself in the morning. I grabbed a towel, wrapped it around my waist, ran up the stairs, and knocked on the door. There was no answer. I knocked a little louder, and Ed opened the door with the chain still attached.

"Yes, what is it?" he snarled.

"You've got to help him, honey. He's hurt," I pleaded.

"Okay, I'll be right down." He was a good man.

THE MEMORIAL SERVICE was held at the house. We stood around the dining table with Ed's urn in the middle directly under the chandelier. Each of us was to say something, even one or two sentences, that reminded us of Ed.

Bambi's husband Jim started things off and at six foot eight, he said simply, "he wasn't tall."

We giggled softly.

Sandi was next. "He always had time to listen."

Next to Sandi was Ilana, who worked with me at the spa. Her big eyes were arctic blue mostly from crying. "I'll always remember his sweet face," she whispered,

After Ilana finished, it was Lis's turn. Lis was with her boyfriend, Ariel. I thought they were perfect for one another because they were the same, small size. "He was so much fun," Lis said, smiling so big that her eyes almost disappeared.

Erick and his girlfriend, Jamdra, worked with Ed at the hospital. They stood next to one another, holding hands tightly to keep from crying. Erick had been a student of Ed's. From the moment they met, they became the closest of friends. Jamdra, or Jammie, which was what Ed called her, was Cuban as were both Ed and Erick.

"He loved the way I rubbed his head," she said.

I looked over at her, and we smiled.

Erick, who was having a hard time holding back the tears, added, "He was the best teacher. I'm going to miss you, man!"

My oldest brother, Steve said, "I finally had a brother who looked like me and now he's gone."

Steve and Eddie did look more like brothers than Steve and I did. Both of them were bald and dark with dark eyes. Whenever we were out with them, people always assumed that Ed and Steve were related, and I was the outsider.

My sister-in-law Susan stood next to Steve, her arm about his waist. Not only were they my family, but they had always been my good friends. Susan started by saying, "Eddie, I am going to miss your even temper and the way you could be objective about anything...except maybe George Bush."

Richard and Jack stood side by side. They were our closest friends since moving to Florida, and I had once worked for them.

Richard had an extremely caustic personality and could cut your throat with the snap of a finger but, if he liked you, then you could do no wrong. Jack, on the other hand, was personable and could talk your ear off.

"He looked the best in a red wig," Richard noted.

We snickered because he was right, Eddie did look good as a redhead.

Jack, always the orator, said, "It was good to meet another couple that had been together for almost as long as Richard and me. We always had such a good time together; we had so much fun. Eddie, my dear, you are truly missed."

My father, who was the only one seated, spoke, his voice

solemn. "He was a good son."

"Yes," my mother agreed, "he was a good companion to our son Chick, and we loved him very much."

I know that being Christian Fundamentalists, my mother, father, and sister were not happy with our decision to have Ed cremated, but they could appreciate our reason that the earth is for the living.

My sister Dawn, holding back tears added, "He always spoke intelligently, without using foul language. Ed's father had always told him that a man shows his lack of intelligence by the use of curse words."

I was the next to speak. I was numb and did not know what to say. Dawn reached over, took my hand, and gave it a squeeze.

"I know that he was loved by everyone at this table, especially by me, but I want to say how much I liked him. I looked forward to coming home at the end of the day because I knew that he would be there. We had such a good time together. He made me laugh."

It started out almost as a whisper then rose a little louder. Bambi was singing:

> Cigarette holder which wigs me,
> over her shoulder, she digs me,
> out cattin' that satin doll.
> Baby shall we go out skippin'?
> Careful amigo you're flippin'
> speaks Latin that satin doll.
> She's nobody's fool
> so I'm playing it cool as can be.
> I'll give it a whirl
> but I ain't for no girl catching me.

She paused as everyone at the table sang aloud the catch phrase from the song, "Switch-e-rooney."

Smiles broke out on every face and with fingers snapping we all finished the song together.

> telephone numbers well you know
> doing my rumbas with Uno
> and that'n my satin doll.

The party began, and there were no more tears for the rest of the evening.

June

JERRY WAS LYING on his bed all by himself. I was out of bed early and as I sat, sipping my coffee, looking at my lone dog, I felt very sorry for him. *Maybe,* I thought, *it was time for him to have a new companion.*

The knock on the door startled me. It was George, but he was earlier than usual.

"I saw your lights on," he said. "I couldn't sleep so I came over to see if you were up and you, um, are."

"Let's go," I said. I was out of the chair and heading toward the front door.

"Wait," George said. "Do you have any coffee?"

I could tell that something was bothering him.

"Sure," I said. "Is everything okay?"

Both of us walked into the kitchen.

"This pregnancy is going to kill me. She is up and down all night long. I don't get a wink of sleep."

He was pacing back and forth in the kitchen. I handed him his coffee, black with one Splenda. He took a big gulp of the piping hot coffee.

"She get's grumpier everyday. She was okay after she saw you, but that didn't last long. She won't even let me touch her. When I come anywhere near her, she pushes me away."

He sighed and with his back to me he said, "I need to get laid."

With my coffee in my hand, I was leaning against the kitchen counter top. "If you want a blow job, all you need to do is ask," I said, laughing.

George turned around and looked me in the eye. "Are you serious?" he asked.

I could not believe what I was hearing. "Of course, I'm not serious!"

"And why not?" he continued.

I started to stumble over my words. I did not know what to say. He just stood there looking at me.

"George, you can't be serious."

"But I am. Who better than you, my best friend?"

"Friends just don't do that," I insisted.

He walked over to me. "Again I'll ask, why not?"

I regretted the words as soon as they left my mouth. "All you straight men just want to get your rocks off."

He grabbed the back of my head and pulled me to him, our foreheads together. "Is that all I am to you, a straight man?"

He was starting to scare me. "No, George, you know better than that. I don't think that at all."

"I know how you feel about me. I see the way you look at me."

George looked me in the eye. I could feel his hot breath on my face as he pulled me closer. He held my arms tight to my body. "*Necesito que hagas esto por mi*," he whispered in my ear. "*Sera nuestro secreto*."

I stopped breathing.

He was right. It was a wonder that no one else saw it, because I thought it was obvious, the way I looked at him. I loved George, but I also liked him. I liked being around him, hanging out with him.

If things had been different and we met in a bar, we would have gone home together. Ed and I slept together the very first night that we met. I liked everything about George. I loved his wife and I adored his children.

What was I going to do? The thought of going down on George had always been in the back of my mind. Sometimes at night, I dreamed of us being together, rolling back and forth in my bed.

My mind was spinning out of control and I felt dizzy. What would Bella think if she ever found out? I looked at George and he was pleading with his big puppy dog eyes.

I would do this for him, but I decided that I would do it on my terms. Both of us were going to benefit from this experience.

My heart was beating so hard that I could hear it in my ears. I placed my coffee cup on the counter, looked George in the eye, and turned him around so that the small of his back rested on the counter. I pulled his tank top up over his head and shoulders and tossed it up on the counter. Slowly, I ran my hand over his chest then down his tight flat stomach to the waistband of his shorts. I ran my fingers around his shorts where I stopped in the back.

Taking my time, I lowered his shorts. His erection sprang to life. I knelt down in front of him, bringing my face close to his body. I inhaled deeply, savoring his clean male aroma. I pulled his foreskin back to expose the head and took it in my mouth.

He tossed his head back and whispered, "Oh, God."

He grabbed two handfuls of my hair as I took in his entire length, my lips resting on his meticulously groomed pubic hair.

The room was electric with our energy. I had not experienced that type of passion in years. I knew that he was getting close by the way he was thrusting his hips, murmuring something in Spanish that I could not understand.

George had entered my house this morning with an agenda, but I was the one in control. He started this, but I was going to finish it. I held on tightly to his muscular thighs as he exploded in the back of my throat. We had both stopped moving and were out of breath when he pulled me up to face him.

With the taste of him still in my mouth, he kissed me full on the lips. "*Gracias,*" he sighed.

THE WHOLE DAY at work, I kept reliving the scene over and over in my mind. It was a thrilling experience, one that left my legs quivering the entire day. It was crazy. Why did I let it happen? As much as I enjoyed it, I knew that it was wrong. Part of me felt guilty that I had sex with a married man, my best friend, in fact. The other part of me was ecstatic, so that I had to keep my erection hidden.

George needed release and he had chosen me, fifty-year-old Chick with the gray hair and wrinkles. I kept telling myself that we were friends, and I was just helping out a friend. That is what friends do, right?

No, that is not what friends do.

If I had asked George to do it for me, would he? No. I just hoped that he would still be my friend.

Oh, no, what did I let happen?

My office phone rang, and I jumped out of my seat.

"You blew me away this morning." It was George.

"That's a fine choice of words," I answered back.

"Ha. You're right. That's funny." He started laughing.

"George, this is going to sound silly, but will you still respect me in the morning?" I was serious.

"Chick, I will respect you tomorrow and forever. You are my best friend. Now stop being so serious. Listen, the reason why I'm calling is Bella wants to have you over for dinner. How is Friday night? Eight o'clock?"

"Friday is okay. What can I bring?" I asked.

"How about some of that great wine you brought last time," George said.

"But Bella can't drink," I corrected.

"Yeah, but we can," he said laughing.

Since putting Thom down, I did not like to leave Jerry alone and whenever I could, I took him with me. I dressed in a pair of light linen slacks, a sleeveless v-neck sweater, and a pair of leather slip-on sandals. I looked well dressed but casual, and the shirt showed off all the hard work at the gym. When Jerry and I walked up the driveway, I noticed a big white Ford F150 truck that I had never noticed before.

I rang the doorbell, and George opened the door. He was wearing the exact outfit he had on the first time I came to his house.

His shirt was completely unbuttoned, and he wore his slip on sandals. Obviously, George had started drinking a little early and was feeling no pain.

"Looking good there, Bud," George said. He whispered in my ear. "My Bella has returned. Her mood is wonderful. She even gave me a little this morning."

He put his arm around my shoulder and led me into the house. Jerry ran to the kitchen to see what he could beg from Bella or the boys.

Dale was sitting in the living room with a drink in his hand. He was wearing white jeans and a light green, short-sleeved shirt that buttoned up the front. Because of his size, everything was tight on him. He was outside quite a bit, and his tanned skin showed off his green eyes. His short-cropped hair had taken on more of a blonde color from being in the sun and blended well with the gray at his temples. He was even sporting an earring in his left lobe. He astounded me when he stood to shake my hand, not just because of his size, but more because of his politeness in standing to greet me.

"Good to see you again, Dale."

My mouth suddenly went dry.

He smiled, still holding my hand.

"What are you drinking?" It was George, in the nick of time.

"How about Jack Daniels and soda?" I didn't even turn around to talk to George. I was more interested in Dale's handsome face.

"Hey, me too," Dale agreed, holding up his glass.

"I told you that you guys had a lot in common," George confirmed as he walked into the kitchen.

There was an awkward silence. Dale and I stood there looking around trying to find something to talk about.

Bella came in to save us from one another. She had changed and was positively ethereal as some pregnant women can be. Gone was the dry, ruddy complexion; her spirits were high and positive.

There was a glow to her that had not been there for some time. She wore no makeup. Her hair was down and since it was curly, very full. She was wearing a long strapless dress with a bright batik pattern. Her pregnant belly filled out the front of her dress. I noticed that she was wearing no jewelry. I commented on it.

"I can't wear anything. I am so swollen," she complained.

"I think you look beautiful, just like a Madonna," I gushed.

"Yeah, you look great," Dale added.

"Oh, you boys are just trying to make me feel good," Bella blushed.

"How much longer do you have?"

"She should be here at the end of August."

"Oh good," I remarked. "You know that's my birthday."

"Maybe she'll come for your birthday. Now you boys just sit down, and I'll go see what's taking George so long with those drinks." She disappeared in a flurry of fabric and crazy hair.

"I heard that you were in Wisconsin. How was the weather?"

"It was beautiful. I even found some time to enjoy it. I had a gym in Madison that I had to close down," he admitted.

"You had a gym there too?"

"Yeah, my partner, well I thought he was my partner, we broke up, so I asked him to buy me out, but he just wanted out."

"That kind of sucks," I consoled.

"It's okay, I guess. I got a buyer so it's not a total loss," Dale shrugged.

George walked into the room with the drinks. "Are you boys playing nice?" he asked, laughing.

Bella came into the room with a tray of hors d'oeuvres followed closely by Jerry. George handed her a drink; a club soda with a splash of cranberry juice and lime.

She raised her glass. "A toast," she announced. "To new friends!"

"I feel like I'm going to be grilled like a cheese sandwich," I admitted to Dale, out of the side of my mouth.

"Me too," Dale whispered back. We touched our glasses together.

"Now you boys get to know one another while George and I get dinner ready. Right, George?" Bella insisted. "I said right, George?"

"Oh, yeah," George choked. He was sitting on the arm of the sofa. He jumped up and both of them left the room followed closely by Jerry, who was very interested in what was going on in the kitchen.

"I don't know who's worse, him or her," Dale commented.

"I do; it's George. He is such a yenta," I answered back.

"Oh, yeah?" Dale asked making it sound like a question.

"Don't let all that straight acting bullshit confuse you. Deep down inside he's all Dolly Levy." We laughed and clinked glasses again.

Dale was very easy going, and I felt comfortable talking with him. I could not keep my eyes off his body. He was so big and solid that he completely filled the chair that he was sitting in. With his large, rough-looking hands resting on his knees, you could tell that he was at ease. There was a casualness to Dale that I found attractive. He looked at me, and we both smiled.

"You have a very beautiful dog," Dale commented.

"Thanks," I answered.

"I heard about the loss of your other one. Are you okay?" he asked. His sincerity touched my heart.

"I guess so. We were together for a long time."

That was all it took to get me started talking. That and the Jack Daniels. I talked about Ed, his illness, and how he died. I opened up about our life together. It was truly cathartic just to sit and talk to someone, and Dale was a great listener. He kept his eyes on me the entire time.

Dale talked about his years in the bodybuilding arena.

"You know," he started, "the healthiest people are in the stands. The contestants are all juiced up, starved, and dehydrated. But I'll tell you, with all that pent up emotion, testosterone, sweat and muscles, well, the sex was great. At least it was with Richard and me."

"Who was Richard?" I asked.

"He was my partner. I'll tell you about him later."

"These guys had sex with one another?" I was curious. I leaned in to get closer to Dale.

"Not all of them, but some of them hardly got off the stage before they were blowing you," he said winking at me, as he placed his hand on my thigh. The thought of some guy on his knees in front of Dale had me excited. As I moved in even closer, he gave my thigh a little squeeze, and electricity surged through me. I wanted to kiss him. I laid my hand on his and moved closer as his face turned to mine.

"You boys want to come in for dinner, or do you want to stay in there and make out?" It was Bella.

"I think I'd like to make out," Dale said softly, almost a whisper.

"Me too," I answered back.

As we stood up, Dale noticed that my excitement had tented the front of my slacks.

"What do we have here?" Dale observed.

"Oh, my God. I am so sorry," I babbled. I was so embarrassed as I turned around trying to adjust myself.

"Here, let me help," he offered as he grabbed the front of my slacks and kissed me on the mouth. I almost soiled myself.

I pushed him away.

"You are some help," I said readjusting my pants.

"You say that now," he teased as he put his arm over my shoulders, and we walked into the dining room.

EVERYONE AT THAT particular Halloween party in Philadelphia will tell you that The Jeweltones were the best girl group that never existed.

The four of us, Thomas, Lou, Eddie, and me with my car's

trunk full of dresses, wigs, make up, and signed photographs, headed to Philly for the annual costume party.

We had had publicity photographs taken weeks before and had relentlessly rehearsed the song, "The Love I Lost," which was originally performed by Harold Melvin and the Blue Notes but had been updated with an eighties dance beat.

The competition was going to be fierce as usual. People came from all over the country to attend the party. Some came to the party as singles, others as a couple, but the most fun were the ones who came as a group. There was a group from New York, and one from Philly, and there was us; the group from DC. Once you became part of a group, you had to swear to complete secrecy. We took this seriously; however, it was all in good fun. Everyone who participated did so with the utmost creativity and cheerful readiness.

Russell had been giving this party for years when his partner, Don Miller, was alive. When Don passed away, Russell decided to keep the party alive for it was the only time that most of us got together during the entire year. When John entered the picture and moved in with Russell, he thought the Halloween party was a bad idea, saying it was a memorial to Don. However, when John finally saw the costumes and how much time and effort was put into them, he changed his mind and jumped into the festivities with both feet.

With the song chosen, we decided on an identity for ourselves, The Jeweltones; a fictitious girl group from the sixties. The idea was to make the same dress in four different gemstone colors. Eddie, who always loved the color red, decided that he would be Ruby, and his wig would be the same color as a young Ann Margaret's. Blue was Thomas' favorite color so he chose to be Sapphire. His dress would be rich with lots of sparkle. Lou, or Penny, took emerald green as "her" color and matched it up with a black, bobbed wig. He simply looked divine. It seemed that the only jewel left out of the crown was diamond, in virginal white, and I graciously accepted the part and color. What would be the design of the dress? Ed thought that the dress should be something like Sandra Dee would wear; to the knee with lots of crinoline and a matching jacket.

"No," Thomas disputed. "It must be long and elegant with a fishtail."

As a truce I suggested both. We all agreed that the dress would start out looking cute and demure and become a bit more sultry and sexy. A basic dress to the knee and a matching jacket was made. Pulled over to sit at the waist was a full skirt with tons of netting underneath to make it puff out. At the appropriate time, the overskirt was to be pulled down to the bottom of the dress and hooked into place. Voila! From kitten to tigress all in one pull.

Of course, we were late. Getting four men to look like beautiful women in one bathroom in less than two and a half hours was a miracle. With autographed pictures of ourselves and our CD ready to go, we entered the party just before the winners were announced and the prizes given out. The DJ, a dyke from Center City, stopped the music, popped our CD into her sound system, and with the aid of her microphone, announced, "Live from Washington, D.C., The Jeweltones!"

The music started off slow, just a tinkle on the piano, as we walked onto the stage. The bass beat kicked in, and the lights illuminated the stage. Everyone could see us, and they were quickly on their feet.

"I can remember hoping," the song started.

With our skirts up on our hips and with a flourish of piano and orchestra, we shimmied the skirts to the bottom of the dress, and the audience went wild! On the video, the boys from New York are on their knees, kow-towing to us.

And a legend was born.

The Jeweltones were only seen one more time; right before Eddie, and I moved from Washington, D.C. to Florida.

BELLA SAT ACROSS the table from me, Dale was to my left and George was on my right. She had taken all the leaves out of the table, so it would be cozy. It was set in a vision of white. With the tablecloth, linens, and plates were all in white with sparkling silver and cut crystal glasses. Everything was first class.

"Bella, where are the boys tonight?" I queried.

"They are at my mom's for the entire weekend," she smiled demurely. "Sometimes we meet half way and do a hostage exchange," she laughed. "We can have an adult conversation and not worry what the kids will hear."

This was going to prove to be a very interesting evening. Dale removed his shoe and started lifting my pant leg with his toe, rubbing my ankle. I looked over at him, and he winked. George had taken Bella's hand and was stroking it lovingly.

"How about some of that wine I brought?" I lifted my glass to George.

"Sure," George complied lifting the bottle out of the ice, splashing some water on the tablecloth. He filled my glass. "Dale?"

"Yeah, sure," he agreed offering his glass to George.

"You'd better be careful. This is the wine that helped us get pregnant," George warned with a smile on his face. Obviously, George had already been drinking the wine for the bottle was half-full.

"Well, if that's the case, I'll have two," Dale emphasized laughing.

"I would love to have some. Chick promised that as soon as I deliver, he will bring over another bottle," Bella said. "I haven't had a drink in six months and probably one glass of wine would make me tipsy."

Does anyone say tipsy anymore? George filled her wine glass with club soda.

"Oh, I think that you will be able to handle it, my dear," George slurred. He held up his glass. "To good friends and to new ones. So boys drink up. There's plenty"

The dinner was wonderful, a traditional Cuban fare of chicken fricassee, black beans with white rice and sweet plantains. Of course, the dinner would not be complete without Cuban bread and butter. We dived into the food, mixing the beans and rice together and slathering the butter on the bread. Later, we would have café Cubano and flan. To hell with our diets! With our bellies full and our chairs pushed back, the conversation flowed smoothly and so did the wine.

"Bella, tell us about you," I said, opening another bottle. "Where are you from? Who are your people?"

"I don't know if I have *people*," she snickered. "There's not a lot to tell really. I grew up in Coral Gables, went to La Salle Academy. We were so bad that we used to get high behind the concession stand by the lacrosse field. One time we almost got caught," she laughed. "There were all these plaid skirts running in every direction; it was hysterical."

"You never told me that," George complained, sounding surprised.

"Yes I did. You don't remember."

She went on with her story. "I went to Miami Dade Community College for a couple of years, but it wasn't for me. I started working at this gym in Kendall, you know, behind the front desk. I watched everybody come and go. I started taking aerobic classes at night and for the first time felt good about myself. The management asked if I could take over a few classes a week, and I jumped at the chance. I started teaching spinning. Then I took a class on zumba, and I was hooked. Everyone was taking my class. I got my boobs done, grew my hair long, and the guys started hitting on me right and left."

"Oh, yeah?" George's eyes were half closed.

"Yeah. Why? Don't you think that someone could find me appealing?" She stood up and pulled her dress tightly to show off her swollen belly. She started laughing. She snorted and that made her laugh even harder. She was acting tipsy. I had heard of a thing called contact high before, but I had never seen anyone get drunk just by being in the same room with people drinking.

George stood up and came over to her. "Bella, I think that you are the most desirable woman I have ever met."

He bent over and kissed the fabric that clung to her tummy. He kissed her hand and tenderly kissed her cheek.

"Oh, George, you are the sweetest." She turned to me. "Isn't he the sweetest?"

"Yes, I can honestly say that George is the sweetest," I replied with a smile. I swore I saw George look at me from the corner of his eye. "This has been such a great dinner, Bella. Let me help clean up. You have done so much. Why don't you go put your feet up, I'll do the dishes."

"And I'll help," Dale chimed in. We both started to gather up the dishes.

"I can't let you boys do that." Her eyelids were heavy.

"Yes, you can, and you will. Now the two of you go into the living room and just relax. I think that we can handle the dishes, don't you, Dale?"

"Yes, my captain," Dale saluted.

I was not prepared for what I saw in the kitchen. To say it was a mess would be an understatement. It looked like someone had dropped a bomb in there. They must have used every pot and pan that they owned.

"Oh my God," I said as I surveyed the war zone. "You better pour us another glass of wine. We are going to be here awhile."

We scraped and rinsed everything that could go into the dishwasher. I started on the biggest pots first. Dale was cleaning off counter tops and throwing trash away. He even had the foresight to set aside glass and cans for recycling.

I actually enjoyed cleaning up after the meal, whether it was the house or because Dale and I were working together. Both of us were very efficient, and the task was not overwhelming. It reminded me so much of having dinner parties of my own with Ed, cleaning up late in the evening after everyone went home.

Dale started to whistle. At first I did not recognize the tune, but it dawned on me that he was whistling, "My Funny Valentine." I looked out the window onto George and Bella's beautiful backyard. The memory was too much for me, and I started to cry softly. Dale came up behind me, wrapped his big arms around me, and started to nuzzle the back of my neck when he noticed that I was crying.

"What's wrong?" he whispered.

I could not say anything, the tears falling into the dishwater.

I sobbed.

Dale turned me around. "Did I say something or do anything wrong?"

I wrapped my arms around his neck, soapy hands and all.

"Oh, no, you've done everything right. How did you know that was my favorite song?" I cried.

"I didn't. It is? I mean, it just came into my mind, and I started to whistle. I always whistle when I'm having a good time."

"Are you having a good time?" I looked deep into his eyes. "Because I am."

"Yeah, I am. Even cleaning up seems like fun," he said, then paused, "especially with you."

"Dale," I began, noticing his eyelashes were very long but they were very pale. "I don't want to scare you but I think that, um, maybe," I could not finish my words for they seemed silly and childlike.

"Maybe what?" I could tell he wanted me to continue. "That maybe you could like me? You want to go steady?"

"Don't make fun of me."

"I'm not making fun of you, I'm making fun with you." His green eyes sparkled.

"I know that it sounds crazy but the first time I met you, at the gym, I knew it. Yes, I could definitely like you."

We were still holding on to one another at the sink, my hands dripping all over him. "Wait, that reminds me, I have been using your gym, and I'm not a member. I haven't paid you any money."

"Maybe we can work something out." He kissed me tenderly on the lips at first, then he became more forceful. He pulled me closer. His tongue examined the inside of my mouth. I did not want him to stop, but I could not face George or Bella again with an erection. I broke off the kiss.

"Easy tiger, let me finish up the rest of these dishes," I said turning back to the sink and looking out the kitchen window. Dale was standing closely behind me with his hands on my waist. I could see our reflection in the window, his head next to mine.

With the last of the pots washed and placed on the rack to dry, and the floor swept, finally, the kitchen was spotless. We walked into the living room where both George and Isabelle were passed out on the sofa their heads back, mouths open and both snoring loudly. We passed by the sliding glass doors to the outside, and both realized that the pool lights were not on.

"Hey, the lights aren't on in the pool, and look the host and hostess are out cold," Dale grinned. "Are you thinking what I'm thinking?"

"Come on," I said, opening the door and stepping outside. Instantly, the humidity took my breath way. "Bella always keeps towels over in here."

I was referring to a big, weatherproof plastic chest that had towels and other pool accessories. I grabbed two and threw one to Dale who, wasting no time, was already down to his white boxer shorts. "Just do me a favor. Please don't dive in head first."

He cocked his head to one side and raised an eyebrow as if asking a question, but he obliged me. He stepped out of his shorts and marched to the shallow end. That is when I noticed he was a true redhead. Acting like a wooden soldier, he kept marching until the water was shoulder deep. He swam underwater and resurfaced by the pool's edge. He was holding himself up by his muscular arms.

"The water is great; are you coming in?" he asked.

"Yeah, sure thing," I started pulling my clothes off.

"Wait not so fast, hot shot" he teased. "How about a little show."

I turned my back to Dale and started to whistle "Hey Big Spender" as I pulled my sweater over my head. As I turned to face him, I swung it in front of me, then tossed it on a patio chair. I flipped my sandals off one at a time. I unbuttoned my pants and slowly pulled my zipper down. All the while Dale encouraged me with catcalls and whistles. I again turned my back to him as I slowly lowered my pants and shorts to the ground, giving him a good look at the ass that I had worked so hard to achieve. I stepped out of my pants and let them fall slowly next to my shirt. With my arms outstretched and a grand "Ta-Da," I turned to face him.

"Now that's what I'm talking about," Dale applauded slapping the pool deck. I walked over and jumped into the water feet first. Dale was right; the pool water was refreshing.

We were standing in waist-deep water. I was leaning up against the side of the pool, and Dale was facing me. I was running my hands over his massive shoulders and chest, feeling the short clipped hair. He took my hand and guided it down to allow me to touch his full erection. I enfolded my hand around it.

"Dale, I would like so much to do this with you, but not here, not in their pool." I took his hand and let him feel my excitement. "Is it okay just to kiss and play for tonight?"

"Anything you want," Dale laughed, half-heartedly. "It's funny, I never would have thought that having someone not want to jump your bones the very first night would be a lot sexier than someone who wants to blow you right now."

"I do want to jump your bones but just not now, okay?"

"Okay," he whispered.

He changed the subject. "That's how I met Richard, I was preparing for a contest: Mr. Wisconsin. I don't know how he got into the room. I was showing my posing routine to a few of my colleagues. The gym was closed but he must have known somebody in the room. I was in great shape, and the routine had been choreographed by one of the best. I had paid enough for him. After the routine, I asked for some feedback and all they could say was, 'don't change a thing'. I saw him sitting there with his mouth wide open. He didn't say a word. I went to the locker room to change, and he followed me. He grabbed my cock and tried to kiss me. I pushed him away."

"What did he do after you pushed him?" He had my attention.

"He told me that he had seen me at the gym and that he thought I was hot." I could tell Dale was getting embarrassed.

"Well, you are," With my hands around the back of his neck, I pulled him toward me and kissed him.

"I did remember seeing him at the gym. He was handsome with dark hair and a pencil thin mustache and goatee." He drew the image on my upper lip and chin. "His body was beautiful, but his technique was sloppy. I saw him with his friends; they were there just to have fun. They had no respect for anything or anybody. He wanted me to take him under my wing and help him create a powerful physique for himself. At first, I thought hell no but then he gave me those big brown puppy dog eyes and I said yes. He asked if he could suck my cock."

"What did you say?" I asked trying not to sound too interested. Unfortunately, my erection gave me away.

"I told him no." He put the emphasis on *I* and on *him*. He raised his eyebrow. I received the message loud and clear. "Not before a contest. I had a rule; no sex for one month before a contest."

"One month?"

"The sexual tension helps with your performance. Do you remember the movie, *The Natural*, with Robert Redford?"

"Yeah." I had seen it many times.

"Remember when Barbara Hershey comes to his room to seduce him. Well, that was to break his confidence and since that didn't work, she shot him."

"That really shattered his confidence," I added.

"Richard asked if he could go with me to the contest, and I said yes, against my better judgment. He was so hot and so young, at least a good ten years younger than me. I found a good seat for him right up front. When it was time and I came out and the music started to play, I couldn't help myself. I went all out. I kept looking at Richard and saying to myself, 'What do you think of these biceps? How about my back? My lats?' I stood center stage, as big as you please, and gave him the money shot. I pressed my thumbs behind my rib cage and pushed my chest out and vacuumed in my stomach. Like this," he demonstrated the pose. Even with a soft belly and after so many years away from the sport, he was still awesome.

"They don't do that anymore. I slowly spread my lats out as wide as possible," He showed me how wide he could make his back look.

"The crowd went wild! Richard was on his feet clapping and whistling. He was in control of the video camera, and he was so excited that he almost dropped the camera. After the show pictures were taken with everybody and he weaseled his way backstage and had his picture taken with me with his own camera. He told me that since I had won, he would take me out to dinner. Any place I wanted.

"I needed to get that tanning crap off me, it's a bitch because it's an oil and the best way to get it off is with baby oil. Then you get in the shower. There I was in the shower lathering up, thinking about Richard, and stroking myself. Then the curtain was pulled back, standing there was Richard in all his glory."

"What happened?" I was out of breath.

"He was beautiful. He asked me if I needed any help and I said yes and he helped me. In fact, he helped me so much we never went out. We just stayed in and ordered Chinese," Dale sighed.

"Don't leave me this way. What happened next?"

"He was a good boy for awhile. He moved his stuff into my place. With the money I made at the contest, I bought the gym. Richard had horrible teeth. I took him to the finest dentist in the area and had his teeth fixed. We had them straightened and added shiny white veneers. Ten thousand dollars and fifteen months later, he looked great. We worked together and worked out together. He stopped being sloppy and cleaned up his diet and about a year later won his first title. He looked so good with his spray on tan and his million dollar teeth that I could not keep my hands off him. Seems like everyone else couldn't either. To celebrate, I bought for us two gold bands to symbolize our partnership in life and in work. We even stood up in front of our families and friends. My parents were not too happy with Richard from the beginning. They asked me to wait to see if I was really sure. I was so in love and so blind. Mom and Dad stood behind my decision. We wrote our own vows and had the minister from the Unity Church bless the union. From that day on, I never took my ring off."

He looked down at his right hand with the ring. He sighed. "I would find his in the bathroom or on his night table, everywhere but on his finger. He started to give young men a little friendly advice. Then spotting them on the squat rack or the incline bench. I confronted him when I saw that he was being just a bit too friendly."

"What do you mean too friendly?" I was starting to feel his pain.

"He would keep his hand on their shoulders while walking to the locker room or touching their stomachs while talking about their abs. My name was on the door, and I didn't like that he was being so intimate with the gym guests, and I told him so. That is when he decided that it was time for him to leave. I asked him to stay for a while and think things through. What I did was book myself a flight from Madison to South Beach for an extended stay. It was winter in Wisconsin, and I needed to get away for awhile, to get some sun and warmth. As soon as my plane landed, I felt better. I stayed at a little art deco place on Collins. There was a great big place to work out on Fifth Street. I started to meet all kinds of big boys. Most of them were into the club scene and were doing drugs, and that was not for me at all. I became frustrated because as much as I liked the weather of Florida, I did not like the South Beach party atmosphere. So I took a little drive up A1A and I found myself here."

"I'm glad you did."

"Me too." He placed his hands on my face, then kissed me.

He stepped back. "I called home and Richard was not there. I found an apartment on the beach and went back to Madison to get my affairs in order. That's funny, huh, MY affairs in order when Richard was fucking every guy in town. I finally tracked him down and asked him if he wanted to buy me out of my contract at the gym and he said no, that he was moving on. I packed up all of the stuff that would fit in my truck and moved here. Bella showed me an ad in the paper for the gym. We had been working together at this gym next to the mall for about six months, and she thought it would be a good idea since it was in her neighborhood."

I found myself liking Dale more and more. I reached out, taking him by the arm, I pulled him to me. I loved the feel of his solid muscles in my hands. I turned him around and started to massage his shoulders and neck.

"Oh yeah, baby, that feels great," he said nearly purring.

"Is this a private orgy or can anybody come?"

It was George. Since he was already in a swimsuit, he took off his shirt and jumped into the pool, cannonball style, right next to our heads. When he resurfaced, he shook the water from his short hair, then walked over, trudging through the pool.

"Bella has the coffee on, and I am dying for flan."

He looked down into the pool at the two of us and said, "I didn't know the water was so cold."

We laughed as we splashed him out of the pool.

When we walked into the kitchen after drying off and getting dressed, Bella threw her arms around both Dale and me.

"Thank you so much for cleaning up. I don't know how to thank you boys."

She kissed both of us on the cheek. I knew that I was blushing because my face was beginning to feel warm. Dale noticed it too.

The coffee was poured into tiny cups. *Cafecita* is what the Cubans call it, and it is served very sweet with light foam on top, or *espumita*. Bella made flan, which is thick custard smothered in a burnt sugar sauce. Both the coffee and the flan could spike anyone's sugar level off the chart. I knew I was not going to get any sleep that night.

Bella quickly became very animated from the sugar. "You know that there are three events that are coming up very shortly. The first is Juan's eighth birthday party. Two weeks later is the Fourth of July. Then last, but not least is Chick's big 5-0 at the end of August."

"What are you going to do for your birthday?" George asked.

"I thought about going to Virginia to see my family. It's been a while since I last saw them. Both of my parents are getting up there in age and I'd like to see them. In fact, the last time I saw them was when Eddie died, and they came down for the memorial."

"Let's get together when you get back. We'll have *lechon caja china* and Cuban music. Make it a real party. How does that sound?" George rubbed his hands together in excitement.

"Sounds great." I could not remember the last time I had a pig roast.

"I live on the beach," Dale interjected. "Let's watch the fireworks from my place. The building has grills and umbrellas. We could lay out by the pool. We could make it a real beach day, grill some burgers and dogs. We could just hang out on the beach or go upstairs and watch them from my terrace, I face the water."

"I could be up for that," I affirmed.

"I bet," George snickered.

Ignoring George, Dale continued, "Do you think that the boys would be okay with the noise?"

"Okay with the noise?" George and Bella sang out at the same time.

"Dale, you forget that boys are all about noise. They would love it. To change the subject but not to change the subject, Juan's birthday is the twenty-third of June and he wants a superhero party. I tried to get him to change his mind but no way. With all the comic book heroes being made into movies, that's all the kids want. The party store is filled with Batman and Spiderman and Superman. Do we know anybody that is big and strong and full of muscles?" Bella asked looking at Dale.

It was Dale's turn to blush.

"Well, umm, I don't know about that," Dale started to protest.

"Oh come on Dale, please, think of the kids," Bella pleaded.

"Come on Dale think of the kids," I said rubbing his head. "I would love to see you in a pair of tights and a cape."

"Please say you will do it," Bella said.

After thinking it over for quite a while; and no doubt figuring he was out-numbered, Dale nodded.

"Thank you, thank you," Bella said as she kissed Dale on his blushing cheek. She whispered in his ear, "I already bought the costume."

"Doesn't Superman have a side kick or something?" Dale asked once we were outside by his truck. We had said our goodbyes to George and Bella and thanked them for having us for dinner. I also wanted to thank them for a very interesting evening but kept that thought to myself.

"Why would he need a sidekick when he can do everything faster than a speeding bullet?" I reminded him.

"Yeah, I forgot." Dale leaned up against his truck and pulled me to him. He rested his hands on the small of my back. "Tell me again why you don't want me over."

"I do want you over. Dale. Don't make me feel bad. I just want it to be right, not right now. Does that make sense?"

"Yeah, I guess so." He lowered his chin and stuck out his bottom lip, pretending to pout like a child.

"Can you get any cuter?"

"I'm not cute. I'm hot!"

"Yes, you are." I put my entire weight up against his body and kissed him. He wrapped his arms around me and reciprocated my kiss firmly. The kiss ended, and I put my head on Dale's massive chest.

I sighed. "I'll see you in the morning. George wants to get to the gym early, and I agreed."

"What time are you going to be there?"

"It's our day off so about eight o'clock."

"See you then."

We kissed.

Dale opened the door to his truck, and the aroma of new car smell was intoxicating. It was one of the Ford models that has a full sized back seat. The interior was immaculate. The seats were made of black leather and looked like recliners. The dashboard was equipped with all the bells and whistles; even a large GPS navigation screen. He climbed in and turned on the ignition; country music started to play. Dale leaned over, buckled his seatbelt, winked at me, closed the door to his white truck and backed out of the driveway.

I tugged on Jerry's leash, and we headed up the street to my house.

I HAD AN Uncle Howard. He was married to my mother's sister, Mary. He was four hundred pounds and very demanding. He insisted on three home cooked meals a day, and Mary was his slave. Even when we were on vacation with them in North Carolina, Mary and my mother cooked and cleaned.

Howard never had a good word to say about anyone. I was not what you would call a sissy boy, but unlike my brothers I shied away from sports and hunting. As a good ol' boy from Virginia, I was taught how to properly shoot a rifle and how to cast a fishing rod. I also rode horseback both English and Western, I was even known to jump on the back of a horse bareback, but that came to a slamming halt when I fell off and broke my arm.

Howard was brutally opinionated, as he discussed, with my parents, how I was going to be spending the rest of life alone without a woman. I didn't know why my sexuality was such a concern of his, but his comments were hurting my parents. I needed to put a stop to it. I went to the local gay and lesbian bookstore and found literature on how to talk to your family about being gay and coming out. The most important issue was what not to say and do. You should not go into the conversation thinking that you are a bad person or that you have done anything wrong. I decided that they needed to know that I was the same person they had always known and loved. They were just going to know me a little bit better.

We talked intelligently, and I gave them plenty of ammunition to use on Howard once the topic of my queerness was ever brought up again. They stood up to the old man, reminding him that they were the parents of a gay child, not him. They were proud of me and if he did not stop gossiping like an old crone, they would cease to be friendly. It worked, for Howard never brought the subject up again.

I UNLOCKED THE door, and Jerry ran in ahead of me. I threw my keys in the bowl on the front table as I always did and hung the leash by the door. I walked to the kitchen and turned on the light.

A door from the kitchen leads to the garage, but for the last two years, it had been a shrine. I had removed and packed away all of Ed's things, from his clothes to pictures, files, colognes. I even kept the bag of personal belongings that he had at the hospital, even his razor. I had everything in precisely labeled boxes. I only went into the garage to do my laundry and since I had a cleaning woman once a week, she took care of most of that.

I opened the door and snapped on the light. It was not a large collection of boxes standing in the middle of the room. I still could not believe, after two years, that one man's life could be stored in a few assorted boxes.

Even with all the wine that I had consumed at dinner, I decided that I needed something more to drink before embarking into the garage. I took a glass down from the cabinet, poured two fingers, maybe three of good Tennessee courage, and added a couple of ice cubes. I walked the two steps down into the garage and across the room.

I circled the pile of boxes.

I took a long sip from the glass, and kneeling down, I ran my hand over one of the boxes labeled *clothing*. Feeling the texture, it felt just like any ordinary dry cardboard box. It was unsealed so I pulled up the four flaps that created the top and reached inside. I pulled out one of his favorite tank tops, red with white piping and a lion on the right breast. I held it to my face and breathed in the aroma that was unmistakably Ed even after all these years.

I took another swallow of Jack Daniels and placed the shirt on the floor next to me. I found a smaller box labeled *photos* and placed it on my lap. I opened the box and reached in, knowing that every time I held an image of him it could break my heart, but I needed to go on.

THE BIOTRONIK LUMOS TD 6518 is the size of a ladies' compact. It is placed under the skin in the upper left of the heart. Wires are inserted into the heart, one to keep the heart beating at a healthy pace, the other to keep the heart from racing out of control. Once the hair grew back over the incision, you could barely notice that Ed was hiding something under his skin that was trying to keep him alive. And it did for awhile.

I was afraid to touch him. Maybe not so much touch him as hurt him. But my big husband was far from frail. There were times I would hold him so tight that I could hear his bones crack. Now when I went to embrace him, my arms barely touched him. At night in bed, before going to sleep, I would give him a light kiss on the lips. I would hear him sigh deeply before he would roll over and eventually fall asleep.

I read everything I could get my hands on concerning people

with pacemakers. I changed our diet. We cut out salt, red meat, alcohol, and dairy. We ate fish, chicken, turkey and filled up on fresh fruits and vegetables, organic whenever possible. I purchased vitamin carriers that were large enough to hold twelve to sixteen pills a day. Along with vitamins, I served up an array of omega blends and branch chain amino acids. I was determined to keep my partner healthy if I had to kill the both of us to make it happen.

One afternoon, late in the day, the house was particularly quiet and the sun was warming through the front windows. We were passing one another in the living room when Ed reached out and touched me. His hands had a way of making the tiny hairs on my body stand up and my heart start to race. We stopped and looked at one another. He pulled me towards him.

"Why don't you touch me anymore?" His eyes were sad.

"Oh, baby, I touch you." I stroked his face. I knew where he was going with this line of questioning, and it frightened me.

"You know what I mean." He took my hand and placed it on his skin over where his device was implanted. "What do you feel?"

"I feel your pacemaker." My hands were trembling.

"No you don't. You feel me. This is me and I need you."

He put his arms around me and pulled me to him. I gently placed my arms about his neck and brushed my lips against his.

"Kiss me," he demanded. I could hear the urgency in his voice.

"I'm afraid."

"Why?"

"That I'm going to hurt you."

"Then hurt me." he crushed my mouth with his, exploring the inside of my mouth with his tongue. My desire roared inside me like a wildfire as I pulled Ed even closer to me, holding him in a vice-like grip.

"That's my boy," he whispered in my ear.

He guided my hand down so I could feel his erection through the fabric of his pants. Because of all the medication, it was difficult for Ed to achieve an erection and, as I was realizing, difficult but not impossible. I looked deeply into his eyes, and we both started to laugh. I think I even blushed because my face became very hot. I laid my head on his chest and kissed the area above his pacemaker.

We walked to the bedroom hand in hand.

For so long I had been keeping my distance from the one I loved the most by keeping him safe. As much as I loved him, I was not loving him. I was keeping him safe like a delicate figurine in The Glass Menagerie. He needed my touch as much as I needed his.

Once inside the bedroom, Ed slowly removed my shirt, pulling it over my head and tossing it on the chair in the corner. He kissed me on my stomach, then, un-buttoning my shorts, he let them drop to the floor. My erection was released when he lowered my white briefs. Electricity surged through me when he kissed the head of my penis, then again as he engulfed the head in his mouth. I held on to the back of his head as I rocked my hips back to front, watching myself slide in and out of his mouth.

The sun was casting long shadows into the room as we positioned ourselves on the bed. Ed was lying on his back, his arms behind his head. I was straddling his thighs. After twenty-three years together, I still loved the look and feel of Ed's body. I knew every inch of him and what drove him wild. He was so ticklish that all I had to do was wiggle my fingers at him, and he would start to giggle.

I repositioned myself between his legs. I lifted Ed's thigh over my shoulder and kissed it. He had lost so much weight after the surgery that his legs seemed very thin. One of the things I loved the most about Ed was his beautiful legs. I ran my hand down the length of his leg feeling the soft hairs. I slowly entered him, making sure not to hurt him very much. I kissed him, slowly at first, then with more urgency.

"I love you, Daddy," my favorite name for him.

"I love you more," he answered back with a smile.

Our lovemaking was always easy and gentle. We were never in a rush to get to the finish line. Even after twenty plus years we still enjoyed the contours of one another's body and how well they blended together. Some people talk about fireworks and the Fourth of July when they talk about making love with their partner. With Ed and me, it was more like Thanksgiving. What I mean is it didn't come around often, but when it did it was always warm and fulfilling. You can call us boring but that was how we liked it.

I missed being inside of him, watching his expression as we made love. It was very natural to be with this man. Afterward, lying in one another's arms, we napped. We were so sheltered in our love that we were unaware of the future. On that beautiful sunny day, we had no idea that was going to be the last time that we ever made love. Soon things started to change for the worst. The pacemaker stopped working, and the doctor insisted that Ed have a heart transplant. He refused and two weeks after our twenty-third anniversary Ed died, leaving me helplessly alone.

THE FIRST PICTURE I removed from the box was in a cheap, wooden frame with the glass broken. Carefully, so as not to cut my finger, I removed the shards of glass and lifted the picture out of its frame. Ed was not quite thirty years old in the picture, sitting on the roof of the Paris Opera House. Someone had left a door open, and we walked out to the most spectacular panorama of the city.

Surrounding the roof were these huge, marble statues, of what we thought to be the muses. Of course, in May, the sky was overcast and dreary, but it made a dramatic backdrop to the photograph. Ed had a full head of dark, curly hair and a moustache. He was wearing a checked sports coat with his shirt unbuttoned past the throat, exposing some of his hairy chest. In my mind, this is how I will always see him. I looked down at the broken frame and noticed that there was a piece of lined paper that was folded up behind the picture. I picked it up and unfolded it. There was some writing. It was a poem that I had written to him after our trip to Europe.

I keep a picture of you,
as a young man
on the rooftop of the
Paris Opera House,
the graying sky is a
contrast to your youthful
expression.
Giant sculptures made
of marble from a long time ago,
but yet it seems
like they were made for you.
My eye is the camera,
I see you and the city
that spans out behind you.
We are young now as we were then.
I keep that picture in my mind
to remind me that you,
were not an illusion,
or a statue on the rooftop
of the Paris Opera House.

How silly could I have been? I wanted to express to him in a few words how I would always love him and never forget him. I did miss him. Sometimes at night I missed him so much that I could not go to sleep and would pace the floor until morning. Images of us together, happy and young, came crashing into the self-protected world that I had built, like my own Great Wall. I saw Ed sick and pale in the hospital. I was there when he took his last gasps of air, still holding my hand and looking into my eyes.

I did not cry then or for the next two years after he was gone. There on the floor of my dirty garage, the tears started flowing down my face with total abandon. I pulled countless shirts out of the box and inhaled his smell, trying desperately to remember everything about him. I sobbed into the clothing, holding nothing back. The years that I showed no emotion for the one person whom I loved the most was now flooded by feelings of every kind; love, remorse, guilt and loneliness. I had cried for everything and everyone else, Hell, I even cried at Kodak commercials. Now it was my turn to cry for Ed because my heart was truly broken. I think I even cried for Thomas and Jorge and Albert and for my beautiful Thom who kept me company after Eddie died.

I spent the whole night going through every box and examining its contents. I saw pictures of us at Christmastime in Virginia with my family. There were old photos of him with his family in Havana. One picture that I liked the most was the one of Ed and his brother, Albert, in Cuba on Christmas day. They had on matching cowboy outfits, complete with six shooters, western hats and boots.

By the time the sun was rising, I had compiled a small box filled with what I could not part with. The rest I decided to give to charity and free up some space in the garage. I was exhausted and stiff from sitting on the cement floor of the garage, but I felt cleansed.

I would always love Ed; he would be with me forever. I knew though he would want me to go on with my life. I stood and stretched, I could not believe that I had spent the whole night out there and that the sun was rising. At one point in the night, Jerry had ventured into the garage and was sleeping on a pile of Ed's clothes. I did not want to wake him so I went into the kitchen and made some coffee.

"I CAN'T DO it," Dale protested.

"What do you mean you can't do it? Of course you can do it."

"Look at me. I feel so stupid."

"I can't keep my eyes off of you." That made him smile. He tucked his chin and blushed.

Dale was dressed like Superman, with the blue tights and the red cape. He looked just like the Man of Steel with the exception of his red hair. We were standing in front of a huge mirror that I had leaning up against the living room wall. Dale was standing in the classic Superman pose: wide stance with his fists on his hips, shoulders back and his chest out. He was awesome. I was standing behind him pretending to adjust his costume so I could touch him.

"You know, the only thing wrong about your look is the color of your hair, and I know just how to fix it."

"You are not going to color my hair, are you?" He knew I was a hairdresser before becoming a massage therapist.

"Not really," I ran out of the room. I had a box filled with all kinds of costumes, wigs, and make up on a high shelf in the garage.

It was a shock to open the door and not see the pile of boxes in the middle of the floor. George and I had delivered them to the local AIDS charity thrift shop in South Beach the day after I went through Ed's things.

I grabbed the ladder, leaned it up against the shelf, and climbed up. The big clear plastic bin was covered in dust. I climbed down, picked up an old dust rag, and was back up the ladder in a flash. I brushed off the dust and opened the lid. Fond memories came flooding back to me.

The first item I came across was Eddie's red Jeweltone dress. It was horribly wrinkled from being stuffed in a box in a hot garage for years and years. I ran my hands over the delicate fabric, and some of the netting gave way due to dry rot, I gently pushed it aside. I came across leopard print fabric, elbow length gloves, fake fur, size sixteen high heels and bags of costume jewelry. I found what I was looking for; black spray hair color.

"I found it!" I exclaimed.

I put everything back almost like it was, replaced the lid, and pushed the bin back to its hiding place. I climbed down the rungs of the ladder, telling myself that I would put it back later.

"This is what I was looking for," I said as I came back into the living room.

"What is it?" Dale was very skeptical.

"Its spray on hair color, and the good part is it washes right out."

I shook the can and heard the sound of liquid splashing around inside. "I haven't used it for a long time so I hope it's still good."

"Me too."

"You are not going to be a sissy, are you?"

"No, I guess not," Dale put his chin down and stuck out his bottom lip. He did this because he knew how it would make me react.

"Aw, Dale, you do this to me every time." I walked over and kissed him on his pouting lip.

He wrapped his big Superman arms around me and kissed me back. "Why don't we just stay here and make super love?"

"Maybe after the party."

"You mean it?"

"Will you let me put the color in your hair?"

"What do I have to lose, except my dignity. Spray away, my captain!"

THE KIDS THOUGHT he was the greatest thing since sliced bread. From the moment he walked in the door, the boys were all over him. The girls, on the other hand, were very cool and aloof. They stayed on one side of living room whispering and giggling to themselves while keeping an eye on the boys.

Everything that Superman asked the boys to do they did, from arm wrestling to tug of war across the pool.

With the rope wrapped around one arm, Dale pulled eight boys into the pool with absolutely no effort. Every time any one of the boys would lose, the girls would squeal with laughter.

Dale didn't break a sweat, even when one of girls with long blonde hair and glasses came up and asked him to arm wrestle with her. He was sitting at the head of the dining table, his opponent on the one end. Blake was her name, and she was known in school to question everything from authority to history. She thought that girls were far superior to boys, maybe not in strength but in intelligence. She strutted up to the table, took her place, removed her glasses, and put her arm on the table. Dale gave a sly wink in my direction, and he too placed his arm on the table.

The contrast between the two arms was hilarious, almost cartoonish. It was a wonder that all the adults could keep a straight face. Dale and Blake gripped one another's hand. The intensity on the little girl's face was fierce.

"When I count to three you push against my hand very hard and try to push it down, okay?"

"I know the rules, Superman," Blake answered very sarcastically.

That was the moment I fell in love with Dale. Seeing him interact with the kids, it filled my heart with joy. I stepped outside and George followed.

"I know the rules, Superman," George imitated Blake perfectly. This made me laugh.

"She is something," I added as soon as I caught my breath.

"Yeah, but I don't know what." He was smiling. "You know, Juan is having a great time. Dale is getting a big kick out of this, isn't he?"

"I thought at first he wouldn't do it, but, you know what? I think he is having a great time too."

There was a loud cheer from inside the house, and we went in to see who the winner was.

"Blake beat Superman. Can you believe it?" It was Aaron, who came running up to the both of us.

"No," his father gasped very dramatically. "How did that happen?"

"She just beat 'em, that's all," Aaron shrugged.

"Poor Superman," I sympathized, my hand on Dale's shoulder. "Would some cake and ice cream make you feel better?"

"No, but a big Jack Daniels would," he whispered between clenched teeth.

While the cake and ice cream were served, Dale and I left out the backdoor. We did not think it right for Superman to be seen eating junk food.

"You have a very pretty house," Dale mentioned as we walked up the driveway.

"Thanks, we went through hell for three years to get it to look like this."

IT STARTED OUT as a small beautification project. We wanted to update the bathrooms and refinish the hardwood floors. I noticed a small amount of mildew in the back closet that even a shellac-based primer could not erase. When we took up the carpeting in the back bedroom, we could not believe our eyes; the floor made of Dade county pine was rotting away. We needed some help and we needed it fast.

There happened to be a construction crew across the street, and I asked one of the workers if he would crawl under my house and take some pictures. He agreed. When we saw the pictures, we were horrified. The main beams under the back of the house were almost completely eroded. It seems that there had been a leak from the shower for years, and we did not know about it. If it were not for the carpeting, someone could have crashed through the floor. The first thing we did was move all our belongings out of that room. We started looking for a contractor that we thought we could trust. We interviewed twelve. Out of those twelve, six showed up to measure and calculate for the estimate. Three sent their bids for us to consider. One was so expensive that we disregarded it and him immediately. The two remaining contractors returned to interview again. Vista Construction and Remodeling was the only business owner to send someone over to discuss the terms of the contract.

AJ was a good-looking Latin man with straight white teeth, and he spoke with a calmness that Ed and I liked from the beginning, but that honeymoon did not last very long. We were introduced to the owner, Benjamin Kaplan, who looked like he was going to die at any moment. He was old and decrepit. He walked with a cane and wheezed like he had emphysema, along with a bad case of the shakes. His bulging eyes made me want to leave the first time I met him, but Ed wanted to hear him out. Plus we did not want to start the whole procedure all over again. Ed reminded me that we were desperate and how much, really, could this small renovation cost us?

We moved out of our home into a small one-bedroom apartment five minutes away. All of our treasured items like the silver and the computer came with us to the apartment. What we wanted to keep was stored in the garage, while the rest was left at the curb to be taken away by the neighbors or the garbage people.

The nightmare began when I came home to what looked like someone driving a truck through the front of our house. There was a huge, gaping hole where the window used to be, and as I walked around the house, every room had windows ripped out along with most of the surrounding walls. I was informed that what I had found in the closet was indeed mold and mildew. By law, the air conditioning vents had to be replaced as well as all the walls and ceilings. The hardwood floors were completely ravaged. The joists and beams were taken out as well, leaving an empty space down to the dirt floor. Our house was raped and left to die. To make matters worse, the company then packed up and did not return until six months later.

Vista would not return our phone calls, even when we threatened legal action. We were frantic and did not know where to turn. We tried hiring other companies to come and finish the work, but everyone, at that time, was busy doing other projects plus Mr. Kaplan had seventy thousand dollars of our money, and we were not letting him get away.

Six months later, our phone rang, and it was Vista Construction, as if nothing had ever happened. They wanted to know if we were ready to resume the work on our house. Were we ready? After six months of ignoring our phone calls and threats, we were ready. We were ready to kill. I was instructed to meet Mr. Kaplan at his office on Monday morning. I was astonished by what I saw when I entered the office. Mr. Kaplan was in a wheelchair, an oxygen canister by his side and a tube in his nose.

"We need to finish this project as soon as we can," he wheezed.

"I would like that, Mr. Kaplan," I forced myself to be calm.

"I have a contract that will see our way to the end of this."

"What do you mean a contract. We already have a contract." I was beginning to get agitated.

"Yes, that was for the demolition. Now we need to write one for the construction," his breath was labored.

"Mr. Kaplan," I started.

"Please call me Ben."

"Mr. Kaplan, our house has been raped by your company, and you have the nerve to tell me that we have to sign a new contract for construction."

"That is correct, sir."

"How much is this going to cost me?"

"Thirty thousand dollars."

"And when do you plan to be finished?"

"If you and your..." he cleared his throat, "partner stay out of our way, eight weeks."

"That puts us at the end of May, Mr. Kaplan. Is that correct?"

"Yes, I believe so," he replied smiling, his yellow teeth showing.

"Let me see that contract."

I added on to the contract that Vista Construction had to be finished by May thirty-first or the contract would be null and void. He was certain that the work would be finished long before that date. I also had an attorney write up a paper that stated that I would like the name and address of all subcontractors that worked on our house. The lawyer said that if Vista Construction did not comply with my letter in six weeks, that they had no recourse with Ed and me. In other words, if they did not give us what we wanted, they were not going to get what they wanted.

They ignored my letter, and we did not have to pay them the extra thirty thousand dollars. Instead, we took that money and found a local handyman who finished our house beautifully. He was crazy, and sometimes I thought I had two husbands because he would stay until eleven o'clock in the evening. I eventually gave him a key and told him to lock up on his way out the door. I always knew it was quitting time for him when he brought out his bottle of rum, and he poured himself a drink.

DALE AND I walked up the steps to the front porch. I took the leash off Jerry, opened the door, and let him run into the house.

"Come in and you can get out of that costume and wash that stuff out of your hair. When you get out of the shower, I'll have a cocktail ready for you. How does that sound?"

"Great," Dale said as we walked into the house. I locked the door and hung Jerry's leash on its hook. We paused in front of the big mirror. "You know, I really had a great time, even with Miss, *I know the rules, Superman*, Blake."

We both laughed.

"Yeah, George said that when she grows up, she's going to make some man's life miserable."

"Or woman's," Dale added.

"You think so?"

"For sure."

I tapped him on the shoulder and motioned for him to follow

me. "Let me get you a towel and a wash cloth so you can take a shower."

We were in the hallway at the linen closet. I reached in and picked out what he needed. When Ed worked at the hospital, he would bring home toothbrushes that were sealed in plastic. We had always kept them around just in case we had visitors. Since we had not had many visitors in the past years before his death, there were plenty. I handed one to Dale.

"Now you may need to wash your hair three or four times to get that color out of your hair, but it will come out... I hope."

"What do you mean, you hope?" Dale stood there wide-eyed.

Smiling, I added, "I was only kidding. Now get in there, Superman, and make it snappy."

"Yes, my captain," he saluted and walked into the bathroom. Before he shut the door, he turned back to look at me and winked.

With the bathroom door shut, I heard the sound of running water as the shower came to life. It took a few moments for the water to get to the right temperature, and I waited until I heard the large glass shower door slide shut. I went to the den and turned on the stereo. Teddy Pendergrass was singing, "Come and go with me."

Nothing could get me in the mood more than Teddy. In the song, he is asking some young woman to go home with him. At first she says no, but he is relentless and will not take no for an answer. Finally, she says yes. She has to say yes because Teddy is so smooth. I sighed.

I walked into the kitchen, took two glasses from the cabinet and filled them with ice. I poured the glasses half full of Jack Daniels. After opening a fresh bottle of club soda, I topped off the cocktails. I walked back to the bedroom, which was right next to the bathroom, and placed the drinks on the bedside table. I took a deep breath, kicked off my shoes, took off my shirt, and dropped my shorts, underwear and all. I opened the bathroom door and stuck my head inside. Dale was rinsing the shampoo from his hair. He must have heard the door open because he turned his head in my direction and opened his eyes. He smiled.

"Do you need any help in there?"

"Sure," he answered back. I stepped inside the room and closed the door behind me.

Later we were lying in my bed. The same bed that I had shared with Ed for years. I was lying on my stomach with my head resting on two pillows, looking at Dale. He was on his side, his hand holding his head up. He was stroking my back softly with the tips of his fingers. Occasionally, he would pause at the light batch of hair that grew on the small of my back and pull on it lightly. His touch caused electrical currents to run through my body, and my skin broke out in goose bumps. This made him laugh lightly.

"What's so funny?" I asked.

"Nothing. I like watching your skin react to me touching you."

"I like you touching me. But, I have to tell you, that I am a little nervous."

"About what?"

"Having sex with you."

"You didn't have any problems twenty minutes ago."

"This is different."

"How so?"

"Because now you are going to fuck me."

"Yeah..." He drew out the word.

"Dale, I have only had sex with one person for more than twenty years. I'm afraid that I..." I could not finish my statement.

"Afraid of what?"

"That I won't be any good," I whispered. "I know it sounds stupid."

"Come here."

"I'm right here." I was still lying on my stomach, and Dale was on his side.

"I want you here right next to me," Dale said patting the area in front of him.

I moved over and slid my body up against his. He slowly placed his massive thigh over my hip and pulled me closer to him. The warmth of his body and his masculine aroma were intoxicating. I could have lain there for hours.

"I love everything about you; your good heart, your gentle spirit and your hard ass." He slapped me on my bottom for emphasis. "Look at us, Chick, we are a couple of hot fucks."

Then he kissed me long and hard. I could feel his erection grow in tandem with my own.

"Move over to the middle of the bed," I ordered. "There is something that I've wanted to do to you from the moment I met you."

"What's that?" Dale cooed.

"You'll find out soon enough," I said with a sly smile. "Roll over on your stomach"

"Mmmmm," he said, then did as he was told.

I reached into the bedside table and brought out a bottle of massage oil. I climbed onto the bed and straddled his buttocks. His physique was magnificent.

"Dale?" I whispered softly.

"Hmmm?"

"I love your legs."

The backs of his legs were full and strong. His butt was hard and round. I poured some oil into the palm of my hand. I rubbed my hands together to warm the oil. The smell of lavender from the oil began to permeate the room. I placed my hands on his firm buttocks.

Dale began to purr. "That feels great."

"I'm glad," I massaged deep into the muscles of his gluteus maximus which was indeed maximus. He squeezed his cheeks together, and they became hard as stone. I placed my hands on the small of his back and leaning forward, I placed all my weight as I slid up to the wide part of his back.

"Your traps are massive."

I poured more oil into my hands. While still leaning over, I massaged the area between his neck and shoulders. My hard cock was resting in the crevice of his buttocks. I gently kissed the area where his butt met the small of his back. I ran my tongue along his spine. I was titillated by watching the hairs on his back rise to my touch.

I moved off to the left of his body and started to work on the right side, pulling and kneading as I moved down Dale's back to his hip. I loved the feel of his body as it gave way to my touch. Moving to the other side, I ran my hands down the left side. Straddling him, this time the other way, I rubbed his hamstrings following the tense striations.

"I can see every fiber of your muscles. It's beautiful," I exclaimed. I leaned forward to massage his calves as I kissed the place behind his knee. Again I found myself rigid and resting between his butt cheeks.

"I like your technique," he teased.

"Now turn over," I whispered as I lifted myself off his back. Standing at the side of the bed, I watched as Dale turned over. He stretched and my mouth watered at the sight of him. My heartbeat in my ears was deafening. I could feel the blood rush to my face as I stared at his erect penis.

He winked and smiled.

His body had a light covering of golden hair. The hair under his arms was slightly darker.

"I like you with some body hair," I remarked.

"It is something kind of foreign to me because of all those years of shaving my body," he mused out loud; running his hands over his chest and stomach.

I went to the bedside table, this time removing water based lube and three condoms. My heart was beating so hard that I could feel it in my throat. My mouth became dry as a bone. I climbed on the bed and sat down on Dale's massive thighs. Our eyes met and locked. I sighed aloud. I lay down on top of him, and we began to kiss. It started softly then became more passionate. He explored my mouth with his tongue. He grabbed the sides of my head as he looked into my eyes.

"God, I want you!" he vocalized eagerly.

It was my turn to smile.

I tore open the wrapper of two condoms and placed them next to Dale. I poured some lubricant in my hand and began to massage Dale's manhood, lying firm against his flat stomach. He propped himself up on his elbows to get a better look at what was going on. I unrolled one of the condoms down, encasing his cock in latex and extra slick lube. I readied myself and once positioned over Dale, I slowly lowered myself onto him. I took my time, stopping every few seconds to relax. With him all the way inside me, I stopped to catch my breath.

"You okay?" he asked, looking at me.

"Oh, yeah," I smiled at him. "More than just okay."

Dale proved to be a powerful and considerate lover. He would take me to the brink of orgasm, then stop to prolong the ecstasy. We were drenched in sweat by the time we were finished. Exhausted and out of breath, we fell back onto the pillows. All we could do is look up at the ceiling and sigh.

"You know what?" I asked.

"What?"

"You're right. We are a couple of hot fucks," I said laughing and rolling on top of him.

"You ready to go again, young man?" Dale asked.

"Maybe, but let me get some rest."

After falling asleep in one another's arms, we did wake up and, like a couple of teenagers, went right back at it. This time I turned the tables on Dale, and I entered him, while keeping profound eye contact. His legs wrapped around my body. It felt natural to be making love to this man. As was to be our norm, he did not disappoint me.

Sometime around midnight, we showered and got back into bed, this time to sleep. We were both on our sides, my back against Dale's chest, spooning style, his muscular arms wrapped around me.

"I have to open the gym in the morning. Wake me at seven or seven thirty," he whispered. He kissed me on the ear, and I fell into a deep, safe sleep with my own personal superman to protect me.

July

AS USUAL, THE Fourth of July was as hot as hell, and the humidity was over one hundred percent but on the beach, a breeze made the day a bit more tolerable. We went over to Dale's apartment, a nice sized, two bedroom on a corner facing the ocean. One bedroom he had set up as an office, while the other had a king size bed and an extra large, flat panel television. Everything in Dale's apartment was extra large, just like Dale. The living room was decked out with big, overstuffed sofas that looked out over the ocean and since his apartment was on the twelfth floor, the view was spectacular.

"Who did you sleep with to get this place?" I asked when I first set foot inside his apartment.

"Everybody," he quipped.

I slapped him on the shoulder and as usual, he feigned being hurt so I had to kiss him on his 'boo-boo'. He took me in his arms and kissed me. We held on to each other for a few moments, just looking at one another. Dale's face was full of character, and I loved to run my hands over his brow, strong jaw, and full sensuous lips.

Dale lived as if he had just moved in. There were pictures still on the floor, waiting to be hung. In the kitchen, boxes of dishes and glassware along with stainless flatware needed to be put away and I took it upon myself to take over that task. It took us a few weeks to finish decorating his place. We bought and put up window treatments. I added a few more pillows to the bed and upgraded all the bathroom linens. Dale even bought a new bed for Jerry, so he could be comfortable when we stayed over.

"Now your place looks like you live here."

"Thanks to you. I am never here, I'm always at the gym and lately, with you, at your place," he answered smiling.

"Maybe we can spend more time here. It's nice."

"Here, let me give you these," he said handing me several keys on a Dale's Gym key ring.

"What are these?" I asked.

He showed me.

"This one is for the front door downstairs, and this is for the door here, and these two are for the backdoor at the gym. Now you don't have to wait for George."

"I like to work out with George. You aren't jealous, are you?"

"No, not a bit," he paused. "Well, maybe a little. I want you to have your own keys. That's all."

"Dale, you are so sweet."

"I know."

"And thank you for being honest with me."

BEFORE THE FOURTH, we had gone to the grocery store and bought everything that kids and pregnant women would love; hot dogs, cole slaw, burger meat, and ice cream.

"When I was a kid in Wisconsin, we used to make homemade ice cream," Dale reflected.

"Me too. In the summer my nasty Uncle Howard insisted on homemade peach ice cream."

"Yum, yum," Dale said.

"Let's give George and Bella a call and see what time they want to come up. It's almost noon and they should be up by now," I said, laughing.

I called the house number, and it rang eight times before George answered the phone.

"Is everything all right down there?" I asked.

"Bella is not feeling very well. She wants to talk to you. Hold on, I'll get her."

Maybe thirty seconds passed by before Bella picked up the extension."Hello?"

"Bella, honey, is everything okay?"

"Chick, I am not feeling up to going to the beach and hanging out in this heat." Her voice sounded hoarse and weak. "I'm sorry but count us out, okay?"

"Hold on a moment," I said. I turned to Dale. "Bella is not feeling well, and she wants to cancel."

"That's too bad. The boys were looking forward to seeing the fireworks," Dale added.

I returned to the phone. "How about we come down and get the boys and keep them up here for the day?"

"You would do that?" she asked.

"It would get them out of your hair, and they were looking forward to seeing the fireworks."

"Let me ask them."

She placed her hand over the receiver, but I could still hear her ask Juan and Aaron if they still wanted to come to the beach. I could also hear their shouts of approval. "Did you hear that? I guess that means yes."

Bella and I figured that the boys needed a change of clothing after hanging out at the pool. Shorts, t-shirts, and flip-flops would be fine. I would drive down to get them by two o'clock, and I would return them after the light show.

When I left Dale to pick up the boys, he was busy making hamburgers.

"I'll be right back," I said as I kissed him.

INDEPENDENCE DAY IN Washington, D.C., was always a spectacular event. The city literally came to a standstill. Even before nine eleven there were more police posted at every intersection than any other day. The National Symphony always set up on the steps of the Capital building. On this particular evening, the late and great Sarah Vaughan was performing.

The afternoon was hot and humid. There was not a breeze to help move the air around. We used to have a saying in D.C. that you could still smell the fireworks on the seventh of July, three days later.

We were not going to go anywhere while it was so hot so we waited until the sun set before we walked down to the Potomac River, a short six block walk from our small Georgetown apartment. Ed and I had decided to pack a picnic dinner of sandwiches, cold chicken, potato salad, and two bottles of cold champagne. An old friend from high school had given me a wine cooler, which could be worn like a backpack, that was great to keep champagne ice cold. We spied an empty pier to set up as our outdoor dining room. Equipped with a plaid blanket and a portable radio set on the public radio station, we were ready for the festivities to begin.

Ms. Vaughan was scheduled to start at eight o'clock and when she took the stage, the first of our champagne corks flew out and into the river. Her voice was dynamic as she sailed through the songbooks of some of Americas greatest composers—George and Ira Gershwin, Cole Porter, and Harold Arlen.

Sitting at the edge of the pier listening to one of the legends of music, drinking champagne, we were in heaven. Anyone seeing the two of us sitting there, holding hands, sipping champagne and eating cold chicken would instantly know that we were young and in love. The pier started to fill up with others just like us; people looking for a quiet place to sit and watch the fireworks without the streaming masses that were surrounding the Capital. But we noticed no one but one another.

Nine o'clock the fireworks erupted as the National Symphony enthusiastically began playing patriotic anthems. We lay down, both of us resting our heads on the wicker picnic basket, sipping champagne now from the second bottle.

Listening to the symphony play "Stars and Stripes Forever" and looking up, watching the colors explode and having them reflecting over the water, you could not help but be in awe. I always have this enormous pride of being an American on Independence Day, especially while listening to John Philip Sousa. Even though Ed was born in Cuba, he said he felt that this was his home, and that his heart too swelled with pride at the sound of The National Anthem.

With the show over, the champagne finished, and the food almost eaten, we packed up our gear and headed home. I had my head on Ed's shoulder as he carried the blanket and I, the basket. It was a glorious evening, a great night to be strolling up Wisconsin Avenue, hand in hand in the city that throws the best Fourth of July parties. Little did we know, the real fireworks were about to begin as soon as we returned home.

JUAN AND AARON were waiting for me on the front porch when I pulled into the driveway. I went into the house to check up on Bella's condition.

"Oh, you poor thing," I gasped as soon as I saw her. She was sitting on the sofa with her swollen feet propped up on two pillows atop the coffee table. She was wearing a light cotton robe that barely covered her pregnant belly. Her head was back resting on a small cushion, a thin line of perspiration on her upper lip. Someone had placed a cold cloth on her forehead.

She looked up with bloodshot eyes."Thanks so much for taking the boys today, Chick."

"No problem, Sweetie Pie," I said. "How do you feel?"

"How do I look? Wait, don't answer that, I don't want to know."

George walked in the room wearing his usual holiday attire of loud Hawaiian shirt and black swim trunks. "The boys have been ready since seven o'clock this morning."

"I'm happy to take them off your hands for a few hours. We'll have a lot of fun. I left Dale making burgers. I'll bring them back after the fireworks, okay? I think we'll walk back because of all the traffic. It'll be easier."

I walked over to Bella and gave her a kiss on the cheek.

"You boys just have fun," she croaked.

"Oh, we will."

I went over and gave George a hug.

"Happy Fourth of July, big guy, and please find a new outfit to wear. I have seen this horrible shirt one too many times," I said, laughing.

"What do you mean horrible? I like this shirt. It's my party shirt," George bragged, holding the shirt open.

"We know, we know," Bella and I groaned at the same time. We all burst into laughter.

"Come on boys, let's go," I called out. Like a herd of wild buffalo, the boys came running down the hallway. They had on their swim trunks and t-shirts. Aaron had an inflatable ring around his waist and a Sponge Bob backpack, while Juan carried his Superman backpack over one arm.

"You can still change your mind, if you want," Bella offered.

"Not on your life." I ruffled Aaron's hair.

When I had the boys comfortably situated in the truck with seatbelts fastened, I beeped the horn and waved good bye to George and Bella as we headed back the eight blocks to the beach.

When we returned to Dale's apartment, he was putting the last of the picnic goodies in a large laundry basket. He was wearing navy blue swim trunks that, if anyone else was wearing them, would have been baggy, but because of his massive thighs, hugged him like a second skin.

"Good Lord!" I exclaimed as soon as I saw him.

"What?"

"Nothing... sometimes you take my breath away."

"Why, what did I do?"

"Nothing, just being you."I kissed him lightly on the lips.

"Hey boys, you can throw your stuff in here."

Dale walked down the hall and showed them the bedroom, where they tossed their backpacks on the bed, opened them, and removed their beach towels. "You guys ready?'

"Yup," they both answered.

"Let's see if Uncle Chick is ready."

I grabbed towels for Dale and myself. Dale picked up the basket filled with the lunch supplies and hoisted it up on his shoulder. The cooler was on wheels and had an extendable handle. All I had to do was let the handle out and pull the cooler along. I locked the door with my new key and, as I turned to walk down the hall, I noticed that Aaron had reached up and grasped Dale's hand. My heart was instantly filled with joy. I stopped and watched the two of them walk hand in hand. Dale was so big and Aaron so small, but they were so natural together as they turned the corner heading for the elevator. When I approached the elevator, they held the doors for me, looking at me from inside. My man and the boys together with me for Independence Day. I was the happiest man on earth as the four of us headed downstairs to the pool.

We had the entire pool area to ourselves. It seems that beach natives go away for holidays like the Fourth, and visitors flock to the overcrowded public beaches. We did not mind being the only people out on the pool deck. Dale started the gas grill located to one side of the deck, and I set out the towels while the boys immediately jumped into the pool.

"You know that looks like a good idea," Dale agreed as he jumped into the water with them, making a huge splash. The boys cheered about the amount of water he displaced.

I kicked off my sandals, threw my shirt on the lounge, and followed Dale into the pool. It was such a hot day, that the water felt especially cool and refreshing. I was floating on my back. Dale obviously gave the boys some secret sign to be quiet, swam under the water, and came up from underneath, flipping me over.

"Hey, what's that all about?" I choked as I re-emerged.

Dale and the boys were laughing. I could not help but to laugh along too.

I started to splash Dale and he, in return, splashed me back. The boys, in their inflatable rings, paddled over to get into the action, and soon the four of us were splashing water all over the place and laughing. Dale and I were acting as much like children as Juan and Aaron.

As we splashed one another, Dale and I stepped closer and closer, causing a great torrent of water around us. Dale stopped and dived under the water and swam over to me and quickly grabbed the bottom of my swim trunks, yanking them down to my ankles. The boys howled with laughter. When I pulled my trunks back up, I swam over to Dale, determined to dunk him under the water. He was trying to run away in waist deep water but was moving slowly. When I caught up with him, I took him by the shoulders and with all my weight, tried to push him under. He was much stronger than I was, but he played along and cried out as I dunked his head. When he came back up, he faced me, took me in his arms and kissed me full on the mouth.

"Oh gross!" both boys cried at the same time.

"You guys act just like Mommy and Daddy," Aaron observed.

"Did you hear that, Daddy?" I joked to Dale.

"I sure did, Daddy," Dale added, then kissed me again. This time there were no protests from the boys.

"Let me get the burgers on," Dale whispered in my ear, not wanting to let me go.

"Anybody hungry?" he asked the boys who answered him with enthusiastic cheers.

"I guess that means yes." He kissed me again.

While Dale busied himself with lunch, the boys and I floated in the pool. Looking up, the sky was bright blue, and there was not a cloud in the sky. It could not have been a more perfect day.

"Uncle Chick?" It was Aaron. He sounded very serious for a five year old. He had floated next to me on his inflatable ring.

"Yes, Big A." That's the nickname I had given him since the day he spelled his name for me. He would always say, *big A, little a, r-o-n*.

"How come you never got married?"

I was taken by surprise. I did not know what to say to Aaron, and I did not want to lie to him.

"Well, Big A," I thought carefully so I would choose the right words. "I was kind of married, for a long time," I paused."He died."

"Don't you want to be married?" he asked. "Aren't all people your age married?"

The questions could have been almost funny, but Aaron was so serious.

"These are big questions coming from such a small boy," I said.

Dale snickered, so I knew that he could hear the whole conversation. "Yes, I would like to be married again. Some day."

"Good. Why don't you marry Dale?" Out of the mouths of babes...

"Yeah," Dale interjected."Why don't you marry Dale?"

"You keep out of this," I glanced in Dale's direction.

"You like him, don't you?" Aaron asked.

"Yes I do, but..." I could not finish my sentence.

"But what?" Again it was Dale.

"Dale, please."

I looked back at Aaron. "Yes Big A, I do like Dale very much and I hope that he likes me too."

"Good, can we eat now?" Juan shouted and we all laughed.

We sat down to lunch. I have to say that the burgers that Dale prepared were about the best I had ever eaten, and the boys agreed. In no time at all, we devoured everything including two bags of potato chips.

We were stuffed and decided to recline on the lounges to let our meal settle. Instantly, we were all asleep and did not wake up until the sun was setting. I looked at Dale who was still snoring loudly, his mouth wide open. I stood up and stretched then leaned over and lightly started to tickle Dale's foot. He began to giggle in his sleep. I tickled a little more, and he laughed himself awake. He looked at me and smiled.

"That was a clever way to wake me up," he chuckled.

"Let's clean up and get the boys bathed. Then we can take a shower. The fireworks will begin in just over an hour."

"Yes, my Captain," Dale saluted.

Obviously, I was sounding a little demanding again.

WITH THE DISHES all taken care of and the boys cleaned and dressed in shorts and t-shirts with the American flag printed on them, Dale and I went into the bathroom to take our shower. It was always a pleasant experience to have someone else wash your back, especially when their hands were as big as Dale's. The shower at my house was considerably larger. I had had it designed around Ed, who was also a big man and it was much easier to maneuver in than Dale's smaller unit, but we made the best of it.

"Oh look, I dropped the soap," Dale said bending over and turning to smile at me.

"We have no time for that, Mister. Remember we have two small boys doing heaven knows what in your living room." I slapped him on his ass.

Living on the beach, there is always a breeze, and tonight was no exception. We were standing on the terrace facing the ocean. Dale had opened a bottle of champagne and poured two glasses for us.

He poured two plastic glasses of ginger ale for the boys, calling it champagne for kids. The boys were very excited to be able to be so close to the fireworks. When the first rockets exploded, they both stood there mesmerized and could only mutter one word, *Wow!*

It was an awesome sight, being so close to the show. Dale had his arm around my shoulder, and I was snuggling against him. Occasionally, he would lean over and nibble on my ear and this would make me giggle. Or maybe it was just the champagne.

Every now and then, I would see the boys looking over at us, and they would whisper to one another or give one another the high five. At one point, when the fireworks were quiet, I heard what Juan was saying to his brother.

"See I told you they're going to get married."

"I know," agreed Aaron. "I'm not stupid."

August

THE BABY CAME early. Luckily, Bella did not have to carry her through the hottest part of the summer. As The Great Chester had predicted, Bella delivered a girl. Just like her mother, she had a full head of curly black hair. I was at work when I received the phone call from George telling me that Bella had gone into labor and that he was taking her to the hospital immediately. I looked at my schedule and found it flexible enough that I could cancel my day and meet them there.

I saw Isabelle's mother Bernice, and the boys, walking toward me in the hospital corridor. They had obviously already seen the baby because when the boys saw me they came running up to me with wide eyes.

"Uncle Chick, Mom had a baby," Aaron said.

"She did?" I asked.

"We saw her. She's gross, all red and stuff. She can't even open her eyes yet."

"That's okay, Big A, I'm sure you were like that when you were born too."

"Yeah, that's what Mom said. Well, bye for now. Grandma is taking us for ice cream."

"See ya," Juan said.

I waved to Bernice as the boys ran ahead.

When I arrived at the room, George and Isabelle were with the baby. George had her in his arms and was lovingly looking at her. I developed a lump in my throat at the sight of my good friend, that I now thought of as a brother, with his new baby. I was extremely happy for George because he wanted a house full of kids. I knew that he loved his boys, but when I saw that tiny baby girl in his arms, I knew he was overjoyed.

"Look how beautiful she is," George said, beaming proudly.

"Thank God, she looks like her mother," I chuckled looking over George's shoulder at the baby. I laid my hand on the back of his neck and massaged it. We stood like that for several minutes, just looking down at her. We both sighed at the same time.

"We have something we want to talk to you about," Bella announced rather seriously. "George, hand me the baby."

George placed the baby in her mother's arms. It was comforting to see George so gentle and careful with such a small, helpless baby.

"Chick, come sit here right next to me," Bella gestured to the chair beside the bed. "I sent Mother and the boys out so George and I could talk to you alone."

"What?" I asked a bit nervously. "You guys are scaring me."

They both looked at one another. George cleared his throat.

"We have decided on a name for the baby," George announced. "We want your opinion."

"Okay," I said, breathing a sigh of relief.

"Actually we thought of you," Bella chimed in.

"You're going to call her Chester?"

"Close but no cigar," Bella laughed. "You are so silly."

"No, but how about Ester?" George spelled it out. "E-S-T-E-R."

I sat there dumb founded looking back and forth between the two of them."You would do that for me?"

"Listen," Bella started, placing a hand on my arm. "Ever since you came into our lives, you have made us so happy. I know that you would have made a great parent. You have filled something that has been missing in our lives for a long time, and I want you to be a big part in this little girl's life."

She handed the baby to me.

Tears started to fill my eyes as I held the tiny bundle.

"What can I say? I feel like I've come back to life because of you, George and the boys, and now you want to name your child after me. I'm honored, but can't you think of anyone else?"

George, who was sitting on the bed next to Bella, stood up. "I've got no one else. Just Bella, the boys, you, and now Ester. Sometimes I think of you as the brother I never had. I love you, man."

The tears started to fall, and I could not stop them. This time they were tears of happiness and not of sorrow. I stood up from the chair and walked to where George was standing. With the baby in one arm, I wrapped my other arm around George and laid my head on his shoulder and wept. He too put his arms around me but instead of crying, he started laughing. Bella slowly and gingerly lifted herself from the bed and slowly walked to where we were holding on to one another. She put her arms around the three of us. What a sight we made.

EVEN THOUGH THE baby had just been born, I kept my plans to visit my family in Virginia for my fiftieth birthday. I wanted just a small gathering of people to help me celebrate half a century.

My mother had asked me what I wanted to eat, and I didn't need to think about it—I wanted Maryland blue crabs steamed with Old Bay seasoning. Eating crabs is very messy and that is another one of the reasons I did not want many people around.

"You guys are going to be okay with Jerry?" I asked George, who had offered to keep him. "He can stay at the house. He'll be all right there."

"Oh, no," George protested. "He's all right staying right here with us."

"I'm going to leave Thursday morning and will be staying for a week. The party is on Saturday because my brother Mike and his wife are leaving for their beach house on Sunday. We'll do something small on Tuesday which is my actual birthday. Are you sure you'll be okay with the dog?"

"Yes, Mother," George crossed his arms and rolled his eyes.

"Oh, speaking of that, my cellular doesn't work on the mountain where Mom and Pop live, so here is their number," I handed George the number on a sticky note. "Just in case you need to get in touch with me."

"When you get back home, we'll have a big party, okay?" George insisted.

"I'm planning on it. Didn't you say that we were going to have a pig roast?"

"Yeah, that's right. I'd better get on that right away."

"I'll talk to you later. I need to go up to Dale's and talk to him. Give him my parent's number and everything."

"Does he have anything special planned for your birthday?" It was Bella, and she was carrying little Ester as she approached us.

"I was hoping that I was going to see my little angel." I took the baby in my arms. I could not get over how much she had changed since they brought her home. The red skin had been replaced by smooth pink skin. Her eyes were open, and I could swear they were looking up at me.

"He says he has a surprise for me."

I looked down at tiny Ester. "Please don't grow up while I'm gone, okay?" I kissed her cheek.

I handed Ester back to Bella. "I will drop Jerry and all his stuff off after work tomorrow. The plane leaves the next day at eight in the morning. Dale insists on taking me to the airport. I told him I would take a cab, but he wouldn't hear of it."

"He's so sweet." Bella cooed.

"Yeah, I know. He's very sweet." I turned to leave. "I'll see you guys tomorrow with my boy."

I found a parking spot in front of the gym. It felt a little odd because for so long, I had entered through the back door, and coming in the front was a whole new experience.

Dale's face lit up as I opened the door. He came out from behind the counter and met me in the center of the room where we kissed hello.

"Hey, baby." I said

"Are you all packed?" he asked.

"Just about. I'm going to take Jerry over to George's in the evening after work. Then I can finish packing."

"I told you I would take care of him. Don't you trust me?"

"Let's not start this again, Dale. It'll be easier to have them take care of Jerry. Besides Bella is home all day long." I caressed the back of his neck.

"I know," Dale placed his muscular arm over my shoulder, pulled me to him, and kissed the side of my face.

"What's that all about?"

"I'm just going to miss you. Is that all right?"

"Yeah, it is." I went to kiss him on the side of his face, but he turned and I kissed him on the lips.

"You are sneaky."

We both smiled.

"Can I call you while you are up there?"

"Oh, I'm glad you said that. My phone doesn't work up there on the mountain, so let me give you their number."

I walked over to the front desk and wrote down my parents' number on one of Dale's business cards. "They are cool. Just tell them who you are, and they'll give me the phone."

"Who am I? Your boyfriend, your lover, or maybe I should tell them I'm the guy you fucked three times last Sunday."

"You pig." I slapped his arm.

"And don't you forget it either, buster." He took me in his arms, pinning mine to my sides and pulled me to him.

"Besides, all you need to do is tell them your name. They already know all about you," I whispered to Dale face to face.

"They do? All about me?"

"Well yeah, pretty much everything. Some things can be left to their imagination. Let's go eat. I'm starving."

Thursday morning came way too fast. The airport had eased up a little on security but I still needed to be there by seven in the morning, which meant we had to leave the house no later than six thirty. The alarm went off, as usual, at five o'clock. I hit the snooze button as Dale snuggled up from behind, his morning erection pressing up against me.

"That's a fine how-do-you-do," I joked.

"Oh, baby, let's just lay like this for five more minutes."

"Ten, if we're lucky."

He pulled me closer to him.

Dale's truck had four doors and a cover over the bed. He insisted that I put my luggage on the passenger seats behind us. We climbed into the cab. The seats were comfortable, and I snuggled down into the leather cushions. He reached into the extra large console between the seats and extracted a CD and inserted it into the player. Soon the rich sounds of Ella Fitzgerald came through the speakers... "My Funny Valentine". He looked for my reaction. Tears came to my eyes. "Why do you do this to me?" I laughed and cried at the same time.

At the airport, we let the red cap take my luggage while we said our good byes.

"I'll be back in a week."

"It will be like forever," Dale answered.

"No, it won't, and besides I will make up for lost time when I get back."

"You promise?" He put his chin down and stuck his bottom lip out like a spoiled child. He did this to me every time he wanted special attention and it always worked.

"What's with the lip?"

"I'm going to miss you, that's all." Dale complained as I kissed his bottom lip. He took me in his massive arms and lifted me off the ground.

"Have a safe flight."

He kissed me firmly on the mouth. An airport police officer was giving us the evil eye so Dale ran to his truck, waved, jumped in behind the wheel, and took off. I stood there and watched his truck get smaller and smaller. I wondered if I should have asked him to come to Virginia with me, but that was water under the bridge.

MY SISTER DAWN met me at the airport.

"Oh my God," she exclaimed. "You look great!"

"Thanks," I said turning around so she could get a full panoramic view.

"Wait 'til Mom and Pop get a load of you," Dawn gushed. "The last time we saw you was at Eddie's memorial, and that was more than two years ago. Everybody will be so excited to see you. Chick, you look ten years younger, I swear."

"Dawn, stop, you are going to give me a big head. Okay, once more, tell me how good I look."

We both laughed.

"We got the pictures of the baby. She's cute. Whose baby is she again?"

"I told you about George. I go running with him and we work out together. Well, actually, it's become so much more than that. We are like brothers. We hang out a lot, go to the ball game, and play with his kids. The boys love me and I think they are something special too. They call me, Uncle Chick."

"All my kids still love you," Dawn said.

"It's like having that time back, you know, when all of the kids were young. Remember how much fun we used to have? Time sure does fly, doesn't it?"

"I can't believe that my baby brother is going to turn fifty."

"How do you think I feel?" I thought for an instant. "Well, actually, I feel pretty good." I laughed.

"And you look really good, almost like you're in love."

"Well, maybe I am and maybe I'm not." I sounded like an eight year old.

"Chester Talbert Ford, you tell me this instant, or I will stop this car!" There was a long pause. The only thing missing was the sound of crickets.

"Dawn, you just sounded like our mother."

"I did? Oh my gosh, I'm sorry. So, tell me."

"His name is Dale and he is a great, big, hunk." I held my hands out wide to give her an idea of his size.

"You mean he's fat?"

"Oh, no. Dawn, he is an ex-bodybuilder and he is gorgeous! He's a red head with freckles. He is so different than Ed." I thought about it for a second. "Well maybe in his looks, definitely, but the way he treats me and the way he loves me is just like Ed. I'm so lucky. In my life I have been truly loved by two men." I sighed.

"I am so happy for you." Dawn reached out and touched my arm.

"Thanks. How are Mom and Pop?" I placed my hand over hers and looked out the window of the car so she wouldn't see how emotional I'd become.

Every time I see my parents, I am surprised at how much they have aged. How did my mother and father become so old in the two years since I last saw them? When I walked into the house, my mother did not even get up from her chair to greet me. I was dumb struck; my mother had gained at least fifty pounds.

"Well Chickie, look at you. When did you start to look like Charles Atlas?" my mother asked, while holding her hands out to beg a hug.

"Charles Atlas?"

"Look at those muscles. Where did you get them?"

"I work hard for these muscles," I bragged as I showed her my best bicep pose.

"Good Lord, boy, come here and give your old mother a hug and a kiss."

I did as I was told. It was not easy putting my arms around my mother, but I bent over, put my hands on her shoulders, and gave her a kiss on both cheeks. She held my face with her arthritic hands so she could study me. She looked deeply into my eyes, her worried face softening into a smile.

"You look good, Chick. We were worried about you for so long and now that I look at you and have my hands on you, I know that you are going to be all right. I love you." She kissed me.

"I love you too, Mom."

"Where is that no good son of mine?" My father said, entering the room. "The only time he calls his family is when he wants to party. Well then, let's party, boy"

One could not help but laugh. Here was my eighty-seven year old father with his plaid shorts pulled up to the middle of his chest and a striped polo shirt buttoned all the way to the top and tucked in. He had on white crew socks with beige, lace-up Rockport shoes. His Shifty Lazar style glasses gave his usual beady eyes a wide-open look, a straw hat covered his bald pate, and he was ready to party? I started to really laugh when he started to dance.

"What's so funny?"

"You are, old man," I chuckled as I walked over to give him a kiss.

"I may be old, but I can still kick your ass."

"There's no doubt in my mind about that, Pop." I kissed him on the cheek. Even with his cane in his hand, he still put his skinny arms around me and hugged me back. I realized that he had started shaking, maybe the beginnings of Parkinson's.

"I love you, boy," he whispered in my ear. Why did that statement always break my heart?

"I love you too, Pop." A tear rolled down my cheek.

SATURDAY MORNING CAME very quickly. As usual, my father and I were the first people awake. Once the aroma of the coffee wafted throughout the house, others started to stir.

My brother-in-law Dick came into the kitchen, followed by his two big dogs; Pete, a black and white German Shorthaired Pointer mix, and Ruben, a great, big, black Newfoundland who I thought looked more like the truffle sniffing pigs from the movie *Hannibal*.

"Good morning, Chester. Good morning, Bernard," he drawled formally. He was all Virginia redneck and proud of it. "I'm going down to pick up the crabs at noon. Chick, you think you might want to tag along?"

"Sure."

Being a man of few words, Dick fixed himself a cup of coffee and with the dogs scurrying ahead, walked out the side door to attend to his morning chores.

He had worked as a union welder for the Federal Aeronautics Association at National Airport but had been retired for a few years. At the age of sixty-six, Dick had the energy of a teenager. While other men would have been humiliated living with his in-laws, he was honored to help; in fact, he single handedly took on the responsibility of taking care of my father after his accident. Pop had fallen four years previously and broken the femur of his right leg. The doctor said that the type of fracture he endured was worse than breaking a hip because he broke the bone at the head. Pop has a steel rod that holds the bone in place but it causes him a lot of pain. He relies on a cane but on an upbeat note, he can predict the weather.

"You know Pop, I can't believe that I'm going to turn fifty."

My father sat there looking out into space. At first I thought that maybe he hadn't heard me.

"Pop," I repeated a little louder.

"I was thinking of that time when we went to that Senators' game. You remember that?"

"Of course I remember. That game made me love baseball that much more. I told you that I made Eddie buy me season tickets to the Marlins. I still keep them. My friend George and I go as much as we can. I told you about George; his wife Bella just had a baby. A little girl that they named Ester."

"I think Dawn showed the pictures. She got a head of black curls?" My father has a distinctive way of phrasing a sentence.

"That's the one. They named her after me."

"That's nice," my father mumbled as he looked out the window.

"Chickie," my mother called in her usual singsong manner. "It's time for you to sing for your supper."

In pink sweat pants and a matching top, she entered the kitchen with the aid of her walker. It was not a typical style of walker, but one that we referred to as the *Rolls Royce* because it was bright red with three wheels, a basket, and hand brakes. In the basket, she had a bag of permanent wave rollers for me to use to set her hair. "I just washed my hair, and all you have to do is roll my hair in these. It should be dry by the time everybody shows up."

"Mother, I haven't set hair in ages,"I groaned.

"Well, I'm sure it's just like riding a bike," she added as she flopped down on a dining room chair, its legs protesting under her weight.

She was right. My fingers knew exactly what to do and in a short time, I had her hair set on the small rollers.

"Thanks, Chickie," she clucked as she and her walker rolled out of the kitchen. I could not believe that I was fifty years old, but my family still referred to me as *Chickie*.

The morning flew by and then it was almost noon. One by one, everybody passed through the kitchen asking me to do something with his or her hair. My father needed a trim.

My sister, bringing in her own box of color, shamed me into tinting her gray roots by saying, "Do you want me to have gray hair in all your birthday pictures?"

My niece Carrie needed her ends trimmed and her daughter Sarah needed layers and like all teenagers, she wanted them *now*.

So, when Dick walked in the side door, I assumed he wanted a haircut as well.

He informed me that it was time to go pick up the seafood for the party. I looked at the clock, and I could not believe my eyes.

On the way into town, Dick had the radio tuned to the country station. Kenny Chesney was singing about how his girlfriend thought his tractor was sexy.

"Do you ever miss it up here?" Dick cut to the chase.

"Sometimes," I answered. "Especially now when the weather is so nice."

It was beautiful where they lived at the foot of the Blue Ridge Mountains. The day was exceptionally clear, and you could see for miles. The mountains, with their distinct blue color, started out a darker shade at the foothills and then became lighter as they grew bigger, almost like someone had torn them out of colored paper and placed one in front of the other. "You guys like it up here, don't you?"

"Love it!" he exclaimed.

"Well, the house will be yours when Mom and Pop pass."

"Don't want it," he said. "Too big. Dawn and I would be happy in a dirt hut, but I like having all those woods for me and the dogs to hunt in."

"You guys would sell the house?"

"Sure. We bought it for Mom because she liked it."

"Where would you go?"

"Stay around here, I guess, or more up the mountain."

He had a distinct redneck vocabulary, but I knew what he meant. I had moved far away to leave my white trash roots behind me, but sometimes I was so comfortable with them that it was scary.

"We're here," Dick announced as we circled in front of the fishmonger's trailer.

The party was supposed to get underway at two o'clock but as soon as we arrived home, I poured the crabs out on the newspaper covered picnic table and dug in. My relatives started to trickle in, getting out of cars in groups of two or more. Some had had to travel as far as two hours to get there.

I was a fine host receiving my guests, kissing them with Old Bay seasoning on my lips. But my family, who enjoyed eating crabs as much as I did, sat down beside me and joined in.

Cracking crabs is very social because you do not get a lot of meat from a crab in one sitting. You have to be patient and, with the proper implements, diligent. It takes on a feeling of a quilting bee, but instead of needle and thread, you use a mallet and pointed knives.

Be advised—do not wear your best clothes because you will get them filthy, or do as my father does, take a clean dishtowel and tie it around your neck like a bib. There are always lots of paper towels available, and you will definitely need them.

The party was in full swing! Everyone was laughing and having a good time. It was a treat to be so at ease with my guests that I could be a mess from eating and no one cared. As soon as someone would leave the seat next to mine, someone else would take his place. I got to catch up with just about every person at the party.

"Someone's coming down the driveway in a big white truck," my cousin Lynne hollered.

"Must be Dean," Dick advised, matter-of-factly. Dean was his youngest son from his first marriage. "Said he was going to get a new truck."

"He must be doing very well because it's one hell of a big truck." Lynne's eyes grew wide to make her point. Dawn got up from her chair and walked in my direction, her camera in her hand.

I could hear the tires on the gravel, but I could not see Dean's truck. I heard the door open, then shut. My father who always sat at the head of the table looked over to see who got out. He slowly pushed his chair back and stood up.

"Good Lord!" I heard him exclaim.

I saw what had made him get up from his seat. It was Dale.

My sister stood in front of me and snapped my picture. "Surprise," she squealed, smiling.

Dale was dressed totally in white. He walked up to my father and introduced himself. He must have asked where I was because my father pointed a gnarled finger in my direction. Dale spotted me, smiled, and waved. He said something to my father that made the both of them laugh, then headed my way.

I stood, covered in crab mess and for the first time since being back in Virginia, I felt like cheap white trash. I ran for the house.

Once inside, I ripped my t-shirt off as I was heading toward the room that I was staying in. I threw the shirt on the floor and as I turned to go into the bathroom to wash my hands and face, there stood Dale.

I burst into tears.

"Oh my God," he gasped. "What have I done?"

"Look at me. I look like a big, messy kid," I sobbed.

"You are a big, messy kid. Now are you going to kiss me or what?" He stepped towards me.

"Don't!" I put my hand out.

"Why not?"

"Dale, look at me. And you're all dressed in white."

"Then I'll take it off," he said as he turned to take his shirt off.

"No, Dale, don't."

"I think he should," said my sister from the doorway. I looked around Dale and saw that the female half of the party had followed

Dale into the house and down the hall. Dale's cheeks flushed bright red.

"I think you should keep out of this," I warned.

"Well," she responded indignantly, imitating Jack Benny.

"Yes, please," Dale insisted. "I would like to have a private moment with Chick if I could. Thank you." He gave them his best smile and they kindly left.

He turned to me."Aren't you glad to see me?"

"Surprised is a better word," I corrected.

"Okay then, aren't you surprised?"

"Yes."

"Then show me and kiss me."

I was so happy to see him, but I was also angry at him and my sister for surprising me like this. I was going to have to get back at her since she knew that I would be a mess, but for now, I was going to kiss Dale.

I washed my face and hands. I kept my shorts on but changed into a clean shirt. Dale was still wearing what he had on, but now he had two red handprints on the ass of his white jeans.

When we walked out the front door arm in arm, the whole party stood and applauded.

"For those of you who don't know," I scowled at my sister. "This is my friend, Dale Rowinski."

I turned to Dale. "I said that right?"

He nodded. I proceeded to introduce him to my entire family. He was charming and gracious, shaking hands with everybody.

"Now," he whispered in my ear, "are you going to show me what this fuss is all about with these crabs?"

We found a place to sit down, and I gave Dale a crash course on cracking crabs.

"Get out of my way, and let a pro show you how it's done," said my brother Mike, and he truly was an expert at eating crabs. He could extract the tiniest morsel out in record time. He also had, in my opinion, a tendency to eat some very scary parts.

He demonstrated to Dale the fine ways of opening a crab, removing the guts, and throwing the garbage to the side.

"Grab her right here and snap it in two. Take your knife and cut down the middle," he illustrated.

Mike was six years older and five inches shorter than me. He loved American history and had a tendency to look like a Civil War general, especially George Custer, handlebar mustache included.

It was fun to watch big Dale, with the daintiest fingers, maneuver around the crustacean. You could see the look of disgust hiding behind a thin mask of amusement. He tried to get the hang of it, but I fed him more from my pile of crabs than he was getting from his. I finally realized that he was enjoying me feeding him anyway.

"Give the man something he can sink his teeth into," Dick announced as he brought a plate of grilled flank steak over to Dale and placed it before him.

"Now that's what I'm talking about!" Dale exclaimed as he devoured the meat with a knife and fork.

Watching Dale interact with my family was a pleasure. He was so at ease and seemed to make it his duty to reach out to everyone at the party.

From across the yard, I observed as he talked to Dick and a small group of men, with a beer in his hand, laughing and occasionally slapping one of them on the back. Every now and then, you could tell that one of the men had asked a question about weight lifting as Dale would pantomime a certain movement that showed the muscle it developed. This would cause the women to scream and whistle catcalls.

"That man of yours is a hunk!" Lynne whispered to me.

"He's a hunk, all right," I agreed. "He's sweet too."

"Look at him with Mom," Dawn observed pointing at Dale who was down on one knee speaking softly to my mother who had her hand on the back of his neck, caressing it. Dale had my mother's full attention for, as usual, he had this way of keeping his eyes only on you as you spoke. I knew she would like him as soon as she saw his red hair. Dale reached in his back pocket and pulled out his wallet. From his wallet, he removed several small pictures. One at a time, he showed them to my mother. By the look on her face and the way she was acting, I knew he was showing her pictures of little Ester. I think he was reminding her that the baby was named for me. She smiled at him and kissed him on the forehead as in a blessing. My heart was full, especially when they both turned, as on cue, to look my way and smile.

"Your mother has asked me to stay here and not go back to my hotel room," Dale said to me once we found time to be alone. The sun was beginning to set and the sky was a brilliant pink. "She even said that I could stay in your room with you, if that is okay with you."

"Dale, when I saw you this afternoon, I almost killed you. I was so embarrassed by the way I looked."

Dale tried to say something, but I stopped him. "Wait a minute, let me finish. I saw in you today how kind and gentle you are with my family, people that you just met. You had my mother eating out of your hand, which is not an easy accomplishment. My sister adores you, and my cousin is in deep lust with you. You have made this day so special. I cannot thank you enough." I put my arms around him, and we kissed.

"I have something I need to get off my chest," Dale whispered in my ear. "I never found a hotel room"

I stepped back with my hands on his shoulders, looked him in the eye, and we both laughed.

"It'll be our little secret, okay?"

We said our goodbyes to my guests. The sun was now gone and all around was pitch black, except for the lights on in the house. It was one of the best days of my life and one of the craziest. Up above the mountain, with not much ambient light around, the stars shone brightly. Outside was a deck that ran the entire length or the house. Dale and I were sitting together on a bench, his arm over my shoulder.

"The stars are nice here, but I prefer them from my little terrace," Dale sighed.

"Me too." We had been sitting outside for quite awhile and my parents had already gone to bed. After all the action of the day, it was nice to just sit and relax.

"Are you ready to go to bed?" Dale asked.

"Yes, I am so tired I could sleep for three whole days," I said, yawning.

"Who said anything about sleep?"

"Dale, this is my mother's house!"

"So?"

"So any little noise and every ear will be turned to that room."

"Let 'em." It almost sounded like he said *fuck 'em*.

I stood up.

"Where are you going?"

"Come with me." I held out my hand. He took it and I helped him to his feet. I opened the door to the living room and led Dale down the hall to the bedroom. "I want to show you something."

"You forget," he smiled, "I've already seen it."

"No, not that, smarty," I said, pointing at the heat register on the floor."They can hear everything from up here."

"I can be quiet...can you?" Dale pushed me onto the bed as he slowly took off his shirt, folded it, and placed it on the register. "Now show me a little Southern hospitality." He unzipped his pants and let them fall to the floor.

The next three days were heavenly. We walked with the dogs through the woods. We made love in the shower. Dawn drove us up the mountain to visit her friend, Bobette, who, at her place, The Country Store, sells handmade quilts, jams, jellies, and canned produce grown from local farmers.

Bobette moved from Manhattan to Virginia after a nasty divorce. Her ex-husband was a drug addict who wasted away most of their life savings. Before he could spend everything, Bobette sold the apartment, left town with her parents and bought a house with a barn and the country store across the street. The three of them needed to start over, and Virginia was just the safe haven they needed. Soon after they moved into the house, they started to renovate the barn to convert it into a studio apartment for Bobette.

According to my sister, Bobette missed the fast-paced city and longed for some friends that she could talk to. They met when, one day, Bobette was sitting on the front porch of the store when my sister pulled into the gravel driveway, Mom and Dawn's granddaughter in the car. The three of them stepped out of the car and on that beautiful, crisp autumn afternoon, Bobette got her wish; a friend. My mother, the queen of the quilts, even left the store with an armload of handmade bed coverings, candy, and preserves.

When Bobette saw us pull up in Dawn's car, she flung open the front door and ran out onto the porch. She took one look at Dale and me and stopped."Finally, gay men! I never thought that I would see gay men again," she exclaimed as she threw her arms around us.

The best way to describe Bobette is handsome. She is tall with a large frame and fine blonde hair cut in a straight bob with bangs. She was wearing no makeup when we met her, just showing fresh scrubbed skin with a small dab of shine on her lips. She wore a long plaid skirt with a white t-shirt and loafers.

Bobette told us her life story over lunch; chicken salad sandwiches on whole wheat bread with homemade bread and butter pickles from The Country Store, and iced tea. What would summer be without iced tea, especially when you're from the South. We sat on a wooden picnic table that Dale and I moved into the shade.

"You know, Chick, I hear so much about you that I feel that I almost know you," Bobette said between bites of her sandwich. "You doing okay?"

"I'm doing great for just turning fifty."

"Fifty? Get out of here. You don't look fifty. Now me, I look fifty and I'm only thirty-eight!"

We all laughed.

"Hey, that wasn't meant to be funny,"she said.

We laughed even harder.

"I haven't laughed like that for a long time. Thank you all for coming to see me. I had a great time," she said as she leaned in the driver's side window, saying goodbye.

"Bobette, thank you for the lovely quilt," I said, holding it in my lap. She had insisted on giving me a gift for my birthday. "I appreciate it very much. You are sweet."

"My pleasure. Now you boys come and visit me whenever you are in town, promise? Especially you, you big hunk of manhood," she said to Dale. He blushed as Bobette squeezed his bulging bicep.

THE EVENING OF my birthday dinner, Dale insisted on paying for dinner. My father would not hear of it and proceeded to remove his credit card from his wallet.

"With all due respect to you, Mr. Ford, I have been a guest at your house, unannounced, I need not remind you, and you have shown me the utmost hospitality," Dale said slowly.

My father, who lately had become hard of hearing, asked, "What did he say?"

"He said, 'Thanks for the good time.' Now let him pay," Dick told him loudly.

We all laughed.

"Well, who am I to argue with a man that size?" Dad said, shrugging.

Again we all laughed.

The next morning Dale had to leave to be back to Sea Breeze by Thursday.

"Do you want me to cancel my flight and return with you?" I asked him.

"That would be nice but I think I have taken up a lot of your time with your family and I think you should have the next two days with them by yourself. Like you said, you don't know how much longer you have with them. By the way, they seem to be really okay with you being gay. At least, they have been very kind to me."

I kissed him tenderly. "They had a harder time with me being a Democrat."

Early in the morning, Dale said his goodbyes. He shook my father's hand, and gave my sister and mother a kiss on the cheek.

He also gave Dick a great big bear hug. "Thanks, pal."

"Thank you, my brother," Dick returned with a slap on the back.

At Dale's truck, I could not help but be a little teary eyed. "I'm already missing you."

"Hey, before you know it, we'll be back together." He took me in his arms and kissed me. I wrapped my arms around him and did not want to let go. He finally stepped into his truck, put the key into the ignition, closed the door, waved and drove off, leaving a trail of dust behind him all the way to the end of the driveway.

"Do you miss him?" Dawn asked behind me. I could tell that

she had been waiting two years for the right time to ask that question.

Dawn was married to Steve when she was seventeen years old. Her first pregnancy ended at seven months with the delivery of stillborn twin boys. She immediately became pregnant with Jennifer. When Jen was a toddler, Dawn found herself pregnant with Carrie. My sister has always taken her career as mother very seriously, and she was totally devoted to her kids. Her husband, on the other hand, was a bad boy, every girl's fantasy and every mother's nightmare. I am sure that Dawn thought that all the children would make up for the ones she lost and that hopefully, they would keep her husband home at night

Steve found himself in trouble time after time. He was even accused of robbing his own tire store. I know this because I was with him when the sheriff placed a gun in the passenger window of the car and told me not to move. With two mouths to feed and one on the way and no real money coming in, Steve enlisted in the Naval Reserves. They loaded up the car with their meager belongings and moved to Tupelo, Mississippi, the birth place of Elvis. Everyone was excited about the move; for once, Steve seemed to be maturing.

It did not take long for Steve to show his true colors yet again. Whether he chose Tupelo or it was chosen for him, it was conveniently located only a one hour drive from an old girlfriend who Steve became involved with again. His interest for his family and his career soon faded, and all he wanted was to bury his puny cock between her legs.

I remember Dawn standing on the front porch of my parent's house. I was just a teenager. It was a cold September evening and her only coat would not go completely around her swollen belly. Jennifer, a toddler, held on to her hand and an old suitcase was in the other.

"Please Mom, I need help," was all she said. Her haggard face looked years older than her age as she cried in my mother's arms.

"Of course I do. Not a day goes by that I don't think of Ed." I answered. We had taken a seat at the big kitchen table which easily sat sixteen people. The main reason that my mother bought the house was that the table came along with the deal. "All I have is my memories of Ed. When you left Steve, at least you had your kids and if Dick should pass away, you still have your kids and your grandchildren. When a gay couple breaks up or the other one dies, all that is left for the remaining partner are their memories together." I paused."Now I'm going to make new memories with Dale."

"He's so different from Ed, isn't he?"

"Yes and no," I said, considering the question. "When you look at him, he is very different; the muscles, his coloring. But when you get to know him, he has that same sweet, gentle nature that Ed had." I teared up. "Oh Dawn, sometimes I feel so guilty falling in love with Dale."

She took my hand. "You deserve every right to be happy," she said, consoling me but tears welling up in her eyes too. "We were so afraid for you for such a long time after Eddie died. That's why Pop insisted that we fly down for the funeral, to see if you were okay. Then it was like you fell off the face of the earth. You stopped calling. Christmas wasn't the same without you."

"I was in a really dark place for almost two years. I didn't care about anything or anybody, especially me. Then a year ago, I woke up and took a look at myself, a good long look at myself, and I did not like what I saw. I decided to take my own life back and that is when I met George.

"Dawn, I don't know what I would do without George and Isabelle and the boys. They brought me back to life and gave my life purpose. After Eddie died, I lost all my self-confidence and self-respect. With exercise and love, George helped me regain my self-confidence, and that's when Dale walked into my life. I don't think that I would have been ready for another, decent relationship if it wasn't for George. I owe him my life. Look at me. If you had asked me a year ago if I thought that I could be this happy I'd have said no."

I needed to change the subject.

"That baby Ester is the spitting image of her mother, crazy hair and everything." I said after a few moments, showing Dawn my pictures of the baby.

"It's good to see you smile, baby brother," she said patting my hand. "Now let me make us both a cup of tea."

GEORGE AND THE boys met me at the Fort Lauderdale Airport. I was as excited to see them as they were to see me. George had parked the car and brought them into the terminal to watch the luggage go around. When Aaron and Juan saw me, they came running over.

"Uncle Chick, did you bring us anything?" they both said at the same time.

"Of course I did, but you have to wait because it's all in my luggage."

George came up to me and gave me a hug. "We sure have missed you."

"How's Bella and the baby?" I asked. "Jerry?"

"Everybody's fine. Looks like you put on a few pounds,"

George said patting my stomach.

"Yeah. Lots of Mom's good 'ol cooking"

"I guess we need to get back to running and soon."

"You bet," I agreed. "Look boys, there's my bag. The one with the pink ribbon on the handle."

Juan turned to me and said, "Uncle Chick, sometimes you are so gay." George and I could not help but laugh. Aaron ran after his brother to help remove the bag from the carousel. Once it was off the belt, they fought to see who would bring it to me.

"Did you have a nice surprise?" George asked, his arm over my shoulder.

"You were in on it too?"

He nodded.

"Wait until you see the pictures. When Dale drove up, I had crab all over my hands and face. I was a real sight. I could have killed my sister. She took my picture and cried out 'Surprise!' I ran to the house to clean up and everybody followed me, especially Dale."

"What happened?"

"What do you think? We kissed. He stayed at my mother's house with me and left on Wednesday morning. Actually he should be home tonight."

"Not to change the subject, but let's talk about our party on Sunday. As you know, Monday is Labor Day, and everyone has the day off, so we are going to party. Even Bella says she is going to have a drink. I ordered the pig. I called The Spa and Greg, Ilana, and Liz are all coming. Scott, we don't know about. It seems half of the neighborhood is coming."

I laughed. He was running off at the mouth.

"I am so glad to be home," I admitted, placing my arm around George's broad shoulder. "Can I ask you a question?"

"Ask me anything."

"Are you a little jealous of my relationship with Dale?"

"What, are you crazy?" he asked, wide eyed. "I think it's great! Dale just adds one more person to our family, well, maybe two."

"Or three," I added, laughing. "I really am glad I'm home."

"We are too," George added, his hand on my waist, as we headed to the car. The boys ran ahead of us pushing my suitcase.

WHEN I WAS growing up our house was deemed The Party House. There was always music playing and at times, people dancing. I can remember my mother and Uncle Carl dancing together, her hair swinging back and forth, the color of fire. They performed a dance something like the Jitterbug. Mother would smile as Carl tossed her out, then brought her back, swinging her under his arm. They looked as though they were having the time of their lives. The music of Benny Goodman often played loudly, and the living room was filled with adults and kids having a really good time.

Since my mother was the youngest in her family, twenty-two years younger than Edna, the oldest, her nieces were just a few years younger and they thought of one another as sisters.

Once, Juanita and her husband, Watson, were dancing off to the side, a cigarette dangling from Watson's lip. You could tell that they were hearing their own music, for they were dancing slowly cheek-to-cheek, Juanita's eyes closed and her expression one of contentment.

Evelyn, Juanita's younger sister, with her Filipino husband, Junior, were a very striking couple swinging one another around the living room floor, Evelyn's skirt lifting and revealing tan hose with white garters.

In the middle of the room was Mother and Carl, their feet moving together in perfect unison.

I remember watching as they would dance in close, then twirl out. My mother, in her pointy toe high heels, would keep her feet moving to the beat. I was counting, "One, two, cha-cha-cha." I took notice of every movement that they made from the spins to the expression on Carl's face.

Years later, I would imitate my neighbor Linda, while my sister performed a perfect impression of our brother Steve, white man's overbite and all.

I could dance like Mom and Carl, I thought to myself.

Once I was sitting there with my ginger ale, pretending I was drinking what the adults called highballs and paying close attention to how they were dancing.

"Chickie," my mother asked. "Do you want to try to dance with Mommy?"

"Oh yes. It looks like so much fun!" I responded in my best grown up, eight year old voice.

The guests stopped dancing so that they could watch my mother and me attempt to dance together. The music started and Mom counted out the beat. "One, two, cha-cha-cha," she directed as I followed her lead.

I was dressed in khaki slacks, a blue short sleeve shirt buttoned up to the neck, and my best Bass Weejuns. I had really wanted loafers. Even at eight years old, I knew that they were fashionable but my father always said that I was just too lazy to tie my shoes.

I stepped on her toes a couple of times, but I quickly

understood the movement and, for some odd reason, I felt the rhythm in my chest, which caused my feet to move in the right direction. The adults cheered and applauded which encouraged me even more. Before long, I had mastered the steps and even tried to spin my mother.

We both agreed that I needed to be a little taller.

The years passed, but I always loved dancing. By the time I was in high school, disco music was very popular. By sixteen I was sneaking into the gay clubs downtown. Even though the clubs were intended for gay men, it seemed like everybody showed up. All dressed, as they say, to the nines. There were women in slinky dresses and high platform shoes, big hair, and tons of makeup. The men had their shirts unbuttoned to the navel with silky pants so tight they had to carry a small bag because there was no room for a wallet. With the music pumping and lights swirling, it was very intoxicating watching the beautiful people move to the beat and I wanted to be just like them.

It even affected the way my friends and I went to school. Never again did the guys settle for ripped jeans and t-shirts; we wore tight bell bottoms and Nik-Nik shirts. Girls were wearing dresses to school again with high-wedged shoes. The guys cut their hair in the new shag style, which was blown dry every day. Everybody wore make up, while girls permed their hair and wore it big and curly. On Saturdays, we would watch American Bandstand with Dick Clark, and every week there was a new dance to master.

I had a friend Pam, who for some reason, her parents called Chippie. We were always practicing the new dance moves after school at her house. We even had our names, in white letters on black t-shirts, with CHIP and CHESTER crossed at the H. On the back of mine was DISCO KID and on the back of Pam's was DISCO BABY.

Our school dances would never be the same again. One Friday night, the music, K.C. and the Sunshine band's, "That's the Way I Like it,"was playing. Pam and I were as ready as we'd ever be. I was dressed all in black, wearing our new CHIP and CHESTER t-shirt. Pam, too, was wearing her t-shirt, with white pants and white high-wedge shoes. Together we made a stunning couple as we danced our asses off. The crowd went wild when we danced the Hustle, Bump, le Freak, and Latin Hustle.

Pam had an Aunt Sadie, who had been an instructor from Arthur Murray Dance Studio for many years. She was so happy to find out that we were serious about dancing that she spent the summer between our junior and senior years of high school teaching the two of us every dance that she knew. We learned the Fox Trot, Waltz, Cha-Cha, and Tango. We soaked all of them up like little sponges. She was unflagging as she showed us the way to hold our bodies and impressed on us the drama of the dance. We spent hours practicing the steps in front of a giant mirror in the living room even practicing our facial expressions.

By the time school started in the fall, we were ready to take on all challengers. Pam and I had a way of incorporating all that Sadie had taught with what we loved about Disco. We combined Tango with Latin Hustle; we added Bump into Cha-Cha. The kids could not believe what they were seeing. In our CHIP and CHESTER t-shirts, we won contest after contest at school. Thirty years later Pam would show me our shirt. She had saved it all those years and actually wore it to our thirtieth high school reunion.

September

THE FIRST WEEK of September in South Florida can be very hot and humid, and the day of my party was no exception. George and Bella planned for the festivities to begin around eight o'clock so they sent out invitations calling for seven. When Dale and I arrived, George was in the kitchen while Bella was nursing the baby.

"Always the first to arrive," George snickered as we walked in the door.

"And usually the last to leave," I finished his sentence.

"Why you boys certainly look handsome," Bella remarked sitting on the sofa with Ester.

"Thank you, kind lady," Dale bowed. "My boyfriend here said I needed something new for his party and who am I to argue."

We laughed as he turned around so Bella could see the whole picture.

"The beans and rice are ready," George announced as he walked into the living room, wearing his traditional party outfit.

"Oh, George! You're not wearing that same old tired Hawaiian shirt and black swim trunks again, are you?" I whined.

"You're not whining, are you?" George looked hurt.

"Yes I am!" I placed my hands on my hips.

"See I told you," Bella nodded to George. "Chick, I told him that you insisted he not wear his usual party outfit, but as you can see, he refused."

"Not if I can help it," I grabbed George by the arm and pulled him down the hallway to his room.

"Chick," George protested, then, feeling my grip as I pulled him down the hall. "Damn, you're strong!"

"Well, you have only yourself to blame."

I pushed him into his room, and then I noticed the black linen slacks and the salmon colored silk shirt hanging from the wardrobe door.

"What's that?" I asked.

I could hear the giggling from the living room and realized I had been double crossed by my friends. George could not keep a straight face and doubled over with laughter.

"You should have seen your face," George cackled.

"I need a drink," I said as I walked out the bedroom door.

"Don't be mad at me," George called.

When I entered the living room, Bella and Dale were trying to stifle their laughter.

"You can both stop now. I could hear you two snickering all the way in the bedroom."

"Oh, baby," Dale walked over to me. "It's your birthday and especially since it is the big five-oh, you should expect your friends to give you a hard time."

He wrapped his big arms around me.

"You're right," I snuggled up against him. "How can I be mad at you?"

I breathed in Dale's warm clean scent.

"I'm going to have a cocktail, want one?"

"Yeah, sure." He kissed me. "Sometimes you can be such a control freak."

"I know. Would you want me any other way?"

"Listen boys, I'll have a drink too," Bella joined in. "I have pumped enough today to take care of Ester until tomorrow, so tonight I'm drinking."

"And what will milady be drinking tonight?" Dale inquired in his best, proper English accent.

"Champagne, my good man," Bella answered affectedly.

Dale and I went into the kitchen to fix the drinks. George had prepared everything. The dinner was simmering on the stove; the bar set up with plastic cups and plenty of ice. Dale headed for the refrigerator to look for the champagne.

"Found it," he announced as he removed a cold bottle of Mumm's Cordon Rouge from the fridge. I filled two glasses with ice and was pouring Jack Daniels when George glided into the kitchen. He was wearing what I had seen hanging from the wardrobe, and he looked good enough to eat.

Both Dale and I stopped in our tracks. George turned around with his arms outstretched so we could get a full view of him. Bella must have picked out the color for him because it was perfect. Dale gave him the wolf whistle. I could not have agreed more.

"Thank you, men, I'll take that as a yes," George replied with a twinkle in his eye. "What are we drinking?"

THE GUESTS BEGAN arriving on time, around eight thirty and the party was in full swing by ten. The temperature had dropped slightly, allowing some of the guests to head outdoors. George had turned on the speakers so that the music could be heard out by the patio. The sun had set, the pig was being devoured and cocktails were being served when George changed the music from soft jazz to Salsa. Couples put down their drinks and started to dance. I looked around, and my eye fell on Bella.

"Would you like to dance?" I motioned to the dance floor.

"Sure. Why not," she replied with a wink to her friends. I whisked her over to the makeshift dance floor. I could not believe that all those lessons from so long ago came right back to me. Even though Ed was from Cuba, he could not dance, and I always said that I had married the only Cuban with two left feet.

When I took Bella in my arms, I looked her in the eyes and we started to move. I admit I was a little rusty, maybe somewhat uncoordinated. But after a few missteps, I fell into the rhythm, and we were dancing like we were professionals. I knew that Bella taught dance aerobics, particularly a technique called Zumba, but I didn't know that she was an excellent Latin dancer.

"Chick, how do you know how to Salsa?" Bella asked.

"I've been dancing since I was a child. First with my mother, then with my friend Pam from high school. You know, Bella, you're not half bad."

She had delivered Ester one month earlier, but she was already back in great shape.

"Neither are you," she responded.

We let the music take over, and we had a fun time on the dance floor. I could not believe that a woman who just had a baby a month ago was dancing as she was. Bella could follow any lead and at the end of each spin, she would kick her leg in a very dramatic way. At one point, I just stood there shaking my hips as she danced around me, vamping me. I even took on the dance face that is kind of like the white man's overbite. I didn't notice that the crowd had grown bigger outside, and were watching us intently. Even George and Dale were outside amongst the guests.

"I think we have an audience," Bella said, looking over my shoulder.

"Oh, yeah? Like Bonnie Raitt sang, 'Let's give 'em something to talk about'."

I spun Bella around six or seven times. I dropped to one knee in a suicide drop, where I hold Bella by the head and she dips all the way to the ground backwards. Every one gasped, then burst into applause.

Bella and I winked at one another. "Madam, may I buy you a drink?" I asked.

"Chick, you were great," Dale beamed. "Where did you learn to dance like that?"

"There's a lot about me you don't know."

"Oh yeah? Something deep and dark?" Dale asked,taking me into his arms.

"Maybe." I left it at that.

"Maybe you'll show me how to move like that."

"Oh no, honey. Either you have it or you don't," Bella remarked coming between Dale and me. She grabbed me by the hand and led me to the side of the pool. George came out of the house, as if on cue, with a birthday cake ablaze with fifty candles. Aaron and Juan followed closely.

"Uncle Chick, do you think that you can blow out all those candles?"Aaron asked nervously. Everyone laughed while I blushed.

"Well, maybe you can help me, okay?"

"You bet!"

George brought the cake and handed it to me. I knelt down so I could be at the same level as Aaron.

"Are you ready?" I asked and he nodded.

"One, two..." at the same time we blew out the candles. Flashes from cameras made me feel like a celebrity. One picture of the boys and me with the multi-candled cake would later rest on my refrigerator.

"Good boy," I said as I ruffled his hair.

The guests started to sing the happy birthday song and Bella took the cake away to be sliced. I stood there holding hands with both Juan and Aaron, looking around at all the guests, my eyes wet with tears of gratitude. I knew these people. They were my neighbors, friends, co-workers, and my new family.

Later, when most of the guests had left, the music changed back to something softer. Dale and I slow danced by the pool. George and Bella joined us and not so much danced but moved slowly side to side, her arms around his neck and his hands resting on the small of her back.

"Did you have fun, Chick?" Bella asked.

"I still am." My head was resting on Dale's shoulder.

"Good," George chimed. "Because we are running in the morning."

"Sure, anything you say," I said dreamily.

ON FRIDAY OF the following week, I arose from my bed and passed the mirror in the dining room. I stopped, turned around, and went back to look at my reflection. Standing naked in front of a mirror one year earlier, I would have been horrified, but today was another story. In front of me was someone younger, leaner, and stronger in so many ways.

I went to the kitchen, fixed myself a cup of coffee, and let Jerry out the back door. When I entered the bedroom, I sat on the edge of the bed and picked up the picture of Ed that I kept by my side of the bed. In the photo, we are on the roof of the Paris Opera house, and he is young and handsome. Every time I think of him, this is the image that I see in my mind's eye. With the picture in my hand, I realized that Ed would always be with me, like an angel sitting on my shoulder. It made me happy to look at this picture. I wasn't sad or lonely anymore when I thought of him. And we could still always talk to one another about anything. There was something on my mind, and I needed him to hear me. It was just like sitting in the den with a cocktail in our hands.

"Eddie, honey," I said to the picture. "I think that I am going to be all right. I have met someone, and I think that you would like him. He is different from you in so many ways, but what he has in common with you, is that he makes me happy. His name is Dale and he is a redhead, not quite a young Ann Margaret, like you in drag, but more of a light titian color mixed with gray. He is a great guy. I want to ask him to move in here with me and Jerry. I've been so lonely, Ed. I want your permission...your permission to go on with my life. Please, say it's okay."

The phone rang. I almost jumped out of my skin.

"Hello," I whispered into the phone.

"Do you remember that lavender lotion you massaged on me?"

"How could I forget," I said, remembering it well.

"That's all I'm wearing..." He cleared his throat. "Chick, what are you doing this evening for dinner?"

My heart skipped a beat and I mouthed the words, *thank you*, to the picture of Ed. "I don't have any plans. What do you have in mind?"

"I want to go to this new French restaurant that is a couple of doors down from my place. The owners joined the gym, and they want to wine and dine me. I asked them if I could bring a friend, and they said, "*Oui*, uh, yes. You up for something like that? About eight?"

"Sounds great! See you tonight." I hung up the phone.

"Thank you, Eddie," I spoke to the picture. "Did you hear what he said? A French restaurant; isn't that a coincidence? I love you and miss you so much."

I opened the bottom drawer of my bed side table and laid the picture down. I struggled with the gold ring that I never removed from my right hand. Once the ring was off, I kissed it and placed it on top of the picture. I closed the drawer.

I leapt off the bed and headed to the den where I let Jerry back into the house. I kneeled down and took the dog's head in my hands "Jerry, baby boy, how do you feel about having a new daddy?" He licked my face as I held him tight. "Yeah, that's how I feel too."

Jerry and I went to the kitchen so that I could prepare his breakfast and as usual, he became extremely animated with the prospects of eating. The morning meal consisted of one scoop of dry food and a third of a big can of dog food. I always added a teaspoon of garlic juice and one fish oil capsule cut in half.

While I was in the kitchen, I opened the cabinet above the oven where we hung all the extra sets of keys. There were so many keys that I did not know to whom they belonged. I recognized my own house and car keys. One set must have belonged to John and Marilyn who used to live next door. They had separated many years earlier because, after John's father passed away, John could not keep his drinking under control. Soon after Marilyn took their son Giovanni to Palm Beach to live with her sister.

I REMEMBER I was standing at the kitchen sink looking out the window when I saw Marilyn dragging two large suitcases toward her car.

She opened the trunk of her car and with great difficulty tried to lift the first piece of luggage. She dropped it and I watched her burst into tears.

I immediately put down my cup and ran for the side door.

"Marilyn, what's going on?" I knelt down beside her.

"I can't take it anymore." Her eyes were red and swollen.

"Talk to me," I pleaded.

"The jury found John's father's condo organization not guilty of neglect."

"That's not right. They should be held responsible."

"The prosecution made it look like John and his sisters were out for money."

"That's ridiculous. That man died because the safety lights weren't working after the hurricane and he fell down the steps and cracked his head. No one found him for twenty-four hours! What a horrible way to die."

"John has been a monster ever since he came back from the trial. He hasn't stopped drinking. Finally he passed out around two in the morning. I've been packing mine and Giovanni's things all morning. Chick, I can't live like this anymore. All he does is drink and yell and pass out. We have a two year old. I need to think about him."

She placed her hand on the bumper of the car and lifted herself up. "I'm going to Andrea's."

She brushed the dirt off her hands.

I loaded the suitcases in the trunk while Marilyn fetched Giovanni. He was still in his pajamas and half asleep when she brought him outside. I opened the passenger side door and pushed the seat forward. She had to peel his arms from her neck to get him situated in the car seat. He woke up and started to wail.

"Papa," he cried. "Where is my papa?"

The sound broke my heart.

"Chick, I have to go. Please see that John is all right."

She handed me her set of keys to their house. "You know I love him very much, but I have to go."

She positioned herself behind the wheel of the car, turned on the ignition, and put the car in reverse. When she stopped to put the car in drive, she paused and looked at me. She blew me a kiss and waved good bye.

I stood there and watched as she took our boy away from me.

"What's going on?" It was Ed approaching from the house. He finally woke up and must have seen the commotion from the kitchen window. I threw my arms around his neck and held him tight.

I had become Giovanni's Godfather after John's friend, Joe, died suddenly of a heart attack.

STANDING THERE, HOLDING onto their keys, I realized that the boy must be a teenager by now. I made a solemn vow to call and see how everyone was getting along.

Then I found what I was looking for; Ed's set of house keys, still on the chain from Disney World. I took them to the back bedroom that we had converted into an office. I found a small, empty gift box that could easily fit in my pocket, dropped the keys inside, wrapped the box in colored paper, and tied it with a bow. This would be my present to Dale.

The entire day at work, I was so excited, even as the minutes crept like hours. I kept looking at my watch. Every time the phone rang, I would jump. I had lots of thing to get accomplished at The

Spa, but my thoughts were on dinner and giving Dale his own set of keys to what would become our house. What would I do if he turned me down? I insistently patted the little package in my pocket, partly to make sure it was still there and partly to give myself some courage. The new me now had time for people and their challenges.

But the phone was ringing nonstop, and it seemed that everything was going to fall apart unless I did or said something about it. In other words, everyone wanted my attention, right that minute! I thought that I had escaped the drama of a beauty salon, but it had followed me into the spa realm. I had just about had enough of it. I called a late meeting that would begin at four o'clock. At the meeting, I informed the staff about the new procedures I had implemented. I still had an open door policy, but they needed to handle some of their own problems. I picked up my cell phone, car keys, and left for the rest of the day. I left the staff standing there with their mouths wide open.

Knowing how my body reacted to just the sight of Dale, I dressed first in tight white briefs. I pulled on a pair of faded boot cut jeans and a long sleeve print shirt.

The restaurant was three doors down from Dale's gym and about nine blocks from my house so I decided to walk. It was the second week in September, and the weather was still hot and humid. A year ago, I would have been completely out of breath and soaked to the skin in sweat. Instead, I had a healthy glow when I stepped into the restaurant. This time, I was not embarrassed by what I was wearing. I immediately recognized Dale by his broad back and shoulders. He was wearing a lightweight sweater and jeans.

"Hello, sexy," I whispered in his ear.

He turned around on the barstool. "It's been a long time since any one has said that to me."

"Someone should say it to you on a daily basis."

"Maybe they will," Dale stood and kissed me on the lips in front of everyone in the restaurant.

The Maitre d' came over to us. He was young, tall, and very blonde. His fine straight hair was cut all one length; it was beautiful. He was dressed, head to toe, in black. "Would you like a table or, perhaps, a room," he said with a sideway smile that reminded me of Drew Barrymore.

"First we'll eat, then get the room," Dale answered back. He held his hand out and shook the young man's hand. "Cash, I want you to meet my friend Chester."

"Chester, any friend of Dale's is a friend of mine," Cash responded holding out his hand to me.

"Please call me Chick." His handshake was firm and friendly.

"Then Chick it is. Come this way please." He led the two of us to a table located in a cozy corner all by itself. "Is this okay?"

"It's perfect," we both agreed at the same time. We looked at one another and laughed.

Dale held my chair out so I could sit. He let his hand brush across my shoulders as he took the seat across from me.

"Chick, can I bring you a drink? Wait... don't tell me. Jack and soda, is it?"

"How did you know? Dale, what did you say?" I asked, my words dying when I saw Dale giving Cash the wink-wink.

"Well, maybe I have been here for awhile before you came in and maybe I told Cash a few things about you," Dale said, blushing.

"What else did he tell you about me?" I asked Cash.

"How about?" Cash offered, holding his hands up to show the exaggerated size of my member.

"Dale!" I cried, punching his arm.

"I'm only kidding," Cash choked. "Dale, you want a refill?"

"Yes, please. Anything to take away the pain of that punch."

Cash turned and left for the bar.

"I'm the one in pain. Hitting you is like hitting a steel pipe." I kissed him where I'd hit him. He took my face in his big strong hands. Pulling me gently across the table, he kissed my lips.

"I feel very comfortable with you," he said, quietly placing his hands on the table palms up. I placed my hands into his. There were so many traits that Dale had that reminded me of Ed, and that was one.

"I do too." This was the time. "I have a little something for you. I reached in the pocket and pulled out the box. I placed it on the table.

"What's this?" He picked up the box and shook it.

"Open it and find out."

I was surprised that he was so gentle with the ribbon. He peeled back the tape and opened the gift without ripping the paper. He cautiously opened the lid of the box and looked inside. His face showed no emotion and my heart sank. Then, ever so slowly, he began to smile and took the keys out of the box.

"What does this mean?" he asked.

"I want you to move in with me," my voice trembling. "I know that it is a big step and of course, you'll want to think it over. Or maybe you just want things to stay the way they are."

"Yes."

"I don't know what I was thinking. Dale, I like you so much." I kept talking

"Chick."

"If you want to keep things the way they are, I can understand."

"Chick!"

"I know you probably want to keep your place. It's a nice apartment..."

"CHESTER!" Dale put his big hand on mine. "Stop talking!"

I swallowed hard.

"I said yes," he whispered.

"Yes?"

"Yes."

He took my hands in both of his. His green eyes were sparkling. "I know that I have big shoes to fill. Ed was a great person. I know that because he loved you so very much. I want the chance to love you too."

My eyes filled with tears.

"I am so happy, Dale. I will say this once, and I'll never say it again. I loved Ed more than anything. After he died I didn't think I could ever love another man. In fact, I didn't want to love anyone ever again. I was told that you only have one true love in your life."

"Do you think that's true?" Dale asked. "That you can only have one, true love."

I thought a moment, then I spoke. "Dale, when I'm around you I am happy. I told my sister that I feel guilty about loving you. There are people out there that never find anybody to love or to love them. Whether they are afraid of getting burned or they just can't give of themselves to really love someone, I don't know. I not only found true love once, but I am lucky enough to find it again...with you."

"You know," Dale started, "I thought that I had found the love of my life, but it was just my dick talking. He was all that I thought I liked in a man. He was tall, dark, and muscular or what I call gay muscular. Really, he was all fake and he had me fooled. Then I met you. Ever since that evening at George and Bella's house, I knew that I wanted to be with you. Chick, when is it my time to have my first true love?"

"Now," I whispered. I knew that this was right. "If you don't kiss me now I'm going to beat you."

"Don't threaten me with a good time," Dale emphasized with a wink. "I like kissing you better." He leaned over the table and kissed me full on the lips.

"Ah-hem," Cash announced clearing his throat. He placed the drinks on the table, along with the menus and left.

"To us," Dale said raising his glass.

I started to laugh.

"Did I say something funny?"

I looked him in the eye and leaned in close to him and smiled. "I was thinking how good your sweater and my pants would look thrown over the back of a chair."

The end

Other Regal Crest books you may enjoy:

Creed
by Michael Chavez

Theo Jaquez comes from a drug infested childhood filled with bad memories and few opportunities. After finding a new life beyond the limits of his birth family, he becomes involved in a series of events that threaten to derail his promising future.

Elijah Bashier is a Moroccan university student wrongfully accused of terrorism and imprisoned in subhuman conditions. Although Elijah is unaware of his paternity, Theo knows exactly who he is and what must be done to honor a promise made to a dying friend. Theo becomes a courier to free the young man and in the process he is charged with unspeakable crimes. Political corruption and young love are at the heart of a sensational trial that ends with the unexpected.

Can Theo keep his promise to a dying friend or will his dark past come back to haunt him and seal his fate?

ISBN: 978-1-61929-053-2

Dark Sorcerer Threatening
by Damian Serbu

A dark sorcerer threatens to expose the existence of a magically concealed kingdom of men who love men. His killing spree endangers King Titian's life, as well as the king's new found love, Phillippe. Romance in the midst of chaos. A burgeoning love, imperiled by black magic. A hidden story from the distant past. In *Dark Sorcerer Threatening,* Titian fights to save his kingdom and the man of his dreams.

ISBN: 978-1-61929-078-5

Secrets of the Other Side
by Eric Gober

Neil Ostwinkle is growing up in a Las Vegas trailer court where he realizes early on that he'd rather marry the Professor, not Mary Ann or Ginger. He prefers Aunt Louise's colorful makeup kits to drab green army men, and he swaps clothes with his best bud Rebecca Mooney because her silky dresses feel like magic on his skin. But in school he learns that being different has frightening consequences and keeps his desires secret.

Neil can't understand why his mom, Ellen, shackles him with one bad stepfather after another. She marries and divorces a mooch, a two-timer, and a pyromaniac. When he hits puberty, he learns you can't always keep your heart from going wild. Or stop your heart from breaking. His first relationships are traumatic, but when Neil meets Clark Martin at a Halloween party, he grabs hold of him tight. Finally, he's convinced love is here to stay, only to discover that AIDS may steal Clark away from him. With help from friends and from Aunt Louise, Neil fights a bitter battle on Clark's behalf. Neil summons help from unusual friends like Jacaranda "Jackie" Stump, a king-sized drag queen with dreams of being a Hollywood wardrobe artist who becomes a friend for life.

Will Neil find and keep love? He comes of age in the Eighties and Nineties, a tumultuous time for a young gay man. Will he be able to make a life of his own when he's battling societal prejudice, family strife, loss, and marriage inequality?

ISBN: 978-1-61929-100-3

CPSIA information can be obtained at www.ICGtesting.com
Printed in the USA
LVOW132309110313

323601LV00003B/7/P